Lotus Blooming

Lorie O'Clare

An Ellora's Cave Romantica Publication

www.ellorascave.com

Lotus Blooming

ISBN # 1419952722

Edited by: Sue-Ellen Gower
Cover art by: Syneca

Electronic book Publication: April, 2005
Trade paperback Publication: October, 2005

Warning:

The following material contains graphic sexual content meant for mature readers. *Lotus Blooming* has been rated *E-rotic* by a minimum of three independent reviewers.

Ellora's Cave Publishing offers three levels of Romantica™ reading entertainment: S (S-ensuous), E (E-rotic), and X (X-treme).

S-e*nsuous* love scenes are explicit and leave nothing to the imagination.

E-*rotic* love scenes are explicit, leave nothing to the imagination, and are high in volume per the overall word count. In addition, some E-rated titles might contain fantasy material that some readers find objectionable, such as bondage, submission, same sex encounters, forced seductions, etc. E-rated titles are the most graphic titles we carry; it is common, for instance, for an author to use words such as "fucking", "cock", "pussy", etc., within their work of literature.

X-*treme* titles differ from E-rated titles only in plot premise and storyline execution. Unlike E-rated titles, stories designated with the letter X tend to contain controversial subject matter not for the faint of heart.

Also by Lorie O'Clare:

Fallen Gods: Jaded Prey
Fallen Gods: Tainted Purity
Full Moon Rising
Lunewulf 1: Pack Law
Lunewulf 2: In Her Blood
Lunewulf 3: In Her Dreams
Lunewulf 4: In Her Nature
Lunewulf 5: In Her Soul
Sex Slaves 1: Sex Traders
Sex Slaves 2: Waiting For Yesterday
Sex Slaves 3: Waiting For Dawn
The First Time
Things That Go Bump in the Night 2004 anthology
Torrid Love: Caught!

Acknowledgements

A lot of research and preparation went into this story. I would like to give special thanks to Rev. Kacey Carlson, who showed incredible patience during recorded interviews, and repeated visits while she instructed me in the ways of witchcraft. Kacey is one of the owners of the 9th Path, which is an awesome store, where I was allowed to browse and learn about so many tools used with this faith. (www.ninthpath.com)

I'd also like to acknowledge Maria Anthony, a wonderful woman I've known for many years, who also willingly shared her knowledge in the Wiccan faith. Her patience in answering my questions is more appreciated than she could possibly know.

The folks at Waxman candles were very helpful in sharing knowledge about Priapus, and actually managed to dig up an old statue of him. (Too bad it wasn't for sale.) They also were able to help in the knowledge of candles, and how they are used with casting different spells. (www.waxmancandles.com)

To all of these wonderful people, I owe my heartfelt thanks!

I've also dedicated long hours of reading research books on casting spells, and several offered "books of shadows" from people I've met in the Wiccan faith while doing this research. Many, many hours have gone into my effort in providing you with this wonderful story, and attempting to keep it as realistic as possible.

Acknowledgements (continued)

The contents of this book are purely fictional. No spell described or recited in this book is real, but has been altered at the recommendation of those who take the craft seriously. Playing with magic is not a game, but a faith. And this author in no way suggests trying anything mentioned in this book "just to see if it will work".

Lotus Blooming

Fallen Gods

Chapter One

Thena Cooke barely noticed the print on the piece of paper in her hand. The words blurred together. Her fingers pressed against the paper, their moistness making the sheet damp.

"I don't understand," she muttered, not talking to anyone in particular.

"I think it's pretty clear." Lynn Holliday rested her wide rear end against the edge of her desk, crossing her arms over her ample chest. "Refusing to work the loader is insubordination and grounds for termination. We can't show favoritism just because of your seniority, Thena."

"I didn't refuse—"

"You were asked to work the loader and you didn't do it. That is refusal. You don't get to choose your machinery. Not on my shift." Lynn stuck her index finger out, gesturing at the paper in Thena's hand. "Sign that and then clear out your locker. I've got a floor to work."

Thena looked at the paper. "Grounds for termination" stood out in bold print, taunting her. The logo for Benn Plastic was on the top of the page. The word "insubordination" made her throat close. She couldn't swallow. Her heart raced in her chest. It was as if slowly the room began spinning around her. She'd worked here for eleven years, ever since she'd moved to Kansas City.

"You're firing me," she said, feeling stupid the moment she uttered the words.

Lynn sighed, turning and reaching for a pen then handing it to Thena. "Your fault. Not mine."

"Paula had a headache. The loader is in a quiet corner." Her arguments wouldn't be heard. She could tell that already.

The form had been filled out, time-stamped two hours ago, right after her shift had started.

After seeing where they were assigned to work, and sensing Paula didn't feel good, Thena had offered to switch machines with her.

"Take some aspirin now. We can do a headache spell over break," she'd told Paula.

Thena's grandmother had always said to keep the balance even, and aspirin often worked as well as the headache spell did.

"You're a gem, Thena." Paula had willingly taken over the loader, where she could sit quietly and sort plastic cups into boxes.

Sure, technically switching jobs required preauthorization, but there was a lot of work to get done, and Thena had figured she would let Lynn know they'd switched machinery when the woman made her rounds. She hadn't expected to be pulled from her work and summoned into the supervisor's office.

Thena looked up, finally taking her eyes off the dreaded piece of paper. She stared at Lynn, into those eyes that she'd sworn for years were empty, carrying no soul. Now she knew the woman had no heart either. They'd worked alongside each other for so long, lived in the same town, and the woman staring back at her showed nothing but hatred.

Hatred for something she didn't understand.

If only she'd seen Lynn earlier that night. Maybe she would have read her emotions. She was getting better at that. Maybe somehow she could have prevented this from happening.

And maybe she wasn't as good as she thought she was.

Thena sighed.

Taking the pen, her hand shook as she scribbled her signature on the paper and then tossed it in the air. Wishing it would fly away, it drifted slowly in front of Lynn while she grabbed for it twice before saving it from floating to the floor.

Lynn wanted to say something. Her mouth twitched, the words right there. Fear and aggravation hardened her expression. She suspected Thena made the paper hard to grab by tossing it, and that embarrassed and infuriated her. She gripped the paper Thena had just signed, turning toward her desk.

"Clean out your locker." Lynn didn't bother to turn around. "And anything you take that isn't yours will be deducted from your final paycheck."

"I'm not a thief," Thena said through gritted teeth. She'd had about enough. "You wanted me gone, so you found an excuse. And it's a pretty lame one. Anyone else and you would have sung his or her praises for being kind enough to swap machines."

Lynn did turn around now. The false smile on her face did nothing but show her wicked satisfaction over what she'd just done.

"You were assigned your job tonight and didn't do it. I don't need to quote policy to you." She puffed out her chest, which gave her a double chin.

But it was the self-righteous look on her face that Thena wanted to slap right off of her. The thought of giving her a nasty pimple on the end of her nose crossed her mind, too.

"You may have others around here intimidated, but not me. I'm not scared of you. Now get your things and get out." Lynn turned around again, moving around her desk although she wouldn't stay there.

No. Lynn would be right out on the floor the second Thena left, bragging how she'd managed to get rid of the witch. And that was exactly why she was getting fired. Too many rumors floated around, and it had Lynn scared. Thena had seen all the signs, and hadn't paid attention to them. The thought of rattling off some kind of hocus-pocus nonsense, just to watch the woman shake in her shoes, entered Thena's mind.

Thena wouldn't waste her time on the woman though. It would be like playing with a brick wall. Lynn had never liked her. And Thena knew she'd started more than one of the rumors that circulated around the factory.

She's scared of you. Scared of something she doesn't understand.

Her factory. Dear God. She'd been working here for eleven years, ever since high school, ever since moving up here from Kentucky. She made good money. She had made good money. Just like that—with nothing more than her signature—she was fired. Unemployed. This just couldn't be happening.

Thoughts of begging, of pleading with Lynn, of grabbing the woman by the neck, of giving her a solid punch in the nose—so many thoughts hit her at once. Her anger swarmed through the room.

But Thena wouldn't make a scene. She knew Lynn would like nothing better than to have her escorted out if Thena threw a fit about being canned. She would throw policy in Thena's face, and she damn well knew the policy. Hell, she'd been here longer than Lynn had.

Thena's stomach tied into knots. There wasn't a lot in savings, some—but how long would it last? Her home was simple, but it was hers. And in a few years it would be paid off. All she had to her name was her car, her clothes, and the furniture in her home. This just wasn't fair!

Maybe you should just become the village witch.

She turned, gripping the doorknob, the metal cold against her sweaty palm, and pulled the door open. The noise of the factory hummed around her. A familiar sound, one she hardly noticed, yet now she heard every sound, the scraping of the machinery, so many voices talking at once.

There was no way she could support herself with the craft. Besides, she didn't believe in making people pay simply because she had a gift. Not to mention the fact that Kansas City was hardly a village.

Her footsteps echoed against the concrete floor as she headed toward her locker, keeping her head up, and ignoring the employees who stared after her with curious looks.

Fired. She's been fired. The old bitch finally fired her.

Tears burned her eyes when she pushed the doors open, her few possessions that she kept at work in her arms. She blinked the moisture away as she headed across the dark parking lot toward her car.

There was no reason to turn and stare at the familiar building once she reached her car. Its structure was nothing impressive, the many windows glowing with light in the night. There was the large Benn Plastics sign that glowed with its neon radiance, flooding the grounds around it with its artificial light. A dark gray sky loomed around the building, the shadows of many trees bordering it.

Standing outside in the night air, its coolness soothing her moist cheeks, she let out a sigh.

"This sucks." And that was an understatement.

Fired for insubordination meant no unemployment. Her savings were meager. And at thirty, a black woman would have her challenges finding another job.

A black woman who has been labeled a witch.

Letting out a choked sigh, she turned to unlock her car as a breeze moved in around her. She welcomed the cool air, the faint smell of the apple blossom trees filling her senses. But there was something else, something stronger enhancing the elements around her. Tossing her things on the passenger seat, she slid behind the steering wheel and looked through her windshield into the night.

A power she didn't understand had seeped toward her. Something strong, something she didn't recognize. Glancing around her, a shiver raced down her spine as she stared harder into the darkness, searching the parking lot, looking for its source.

She slid her key into the ignition as something caught her eye. A figure on the sidewalk alongside the parking lot—someone stood there watching her. In the darkness the person was nothing more than a black silhouette, conveniently masked by the night. Yet he watched her. She wouldn't feel all this power if he hadn't wanted her to sense him. With that much power, he would be able to control its direction. And he was directing it straight at her.

And yes, it was a man. Thena could feel his masculinity, a raw carnal power that soaked the air around her with his strength. Whoever stood there had strong enough powers that she sensed them inside her car, strong enough that he hovered around her, even though he stood so far away.

Her heart started racing and she realized her fingers trembled as she closed her door slowly and quietly. A force that dwarfed anything she'd ever experienced before made it hard to breathe. What kind of being loomed outside on the edge of the parking lot?

Thena knew things weren't always as they appeared. There were powers that lingered around people that most completely ignored. Humans worked to manipulate the spirits, but what many didn't realize was that the spirits could manipulate humans too.

Ever since childhood, Thena had worked to fine-tune her senses, become one with the elements around her. The gift had been passed down, running thick in her blood. Her mother practiced the craft, as did her mother before her. Thena hadn't given much thought to it, but had simply worked to strengthen the gift inside herself too.

Right now it seemed to be working just fine. If only it had been helpful in saving her job.

Thena's hands shook when she pulled out of her stall. The man standing on the sidewalk hadn't moved. He was no more than a dark silhouette, grabbing her attention.

"Who are you?" she whispered, glancing up to notice the waning moon and wondering if she would get an answer.

He continued to stand there as she pulled out of the parking lot and headed toward her house. Suddenly losing her job didn't seem as important to her as figuring out who he was.

Lost in thought, she drove in silence until she pulled into her driveway. The energy around her had calmed. No longer did she sense an unyielding power.

"Maybe I overreacted from being fired." And that would make sense. The strength she'd felt had been too strong.

Fired. She'd been fired. The lump in her throat grew and tears burned her eyes while a rock twisted in her stomach that she couldn't make go away.

Even though she no longer sensed the extent of his power, her own emotions filled the air, moving past her car toward the street. The whole thing pissed her off. It wasn't fair. Thoughts of fighting it, of filing a discrimination claim against Benn Plastics entered her mind.

But she'd moved to Kansas City to start a new life. She wanted to fit in, not live on the edge of a society who basically feared and rejected her.

A witch. Voodoo lover. Weirdo. She'd heard it all of her life. And she'd learned if she kept a low profile, she could walk among everyone else without being patronized.

"Except that I keep slipping," she grumbled to herself, grabbing her things from the passenger seat and getting out of her car.

No matter how hard she tried to just be normal, inevitably someone would have a problem, not feel well, or need guidance, and she hadn't been able to keep her mouth shut. After eleven years in Kansas City, once again, she was known as the "village witch".

That wouldn't be a bad thing except that it deemed her unapproachable. Why couldn't she just be known as Thena Cooke? All she wanted was to be appreciated for who she was, an intelligent woman who was loving and caring. Not some strange person to be muttered about and left alone.

Her temper soured as she headed toward her house. Never had she been so infuriated with her circumstances. And it was possibly that outrage that prevented her from feeling the returning power that floated into her neighborhood.

Priapus stood at the corner, alone on the quiet street, watching while Thena got out of her car and headed into her home. His overcoat hung past his knees, covering his large frame, obscuring any details that might be identified in the dark.

Not that there was anyone outside at this hour on the quiet residential street. Decent, hardworking people lived in these homes, all tucked in for the night. He was very much alone, which was for the best. Too many centuries had passed since he'd walked on this planet. No one would recognize him, not in this country, not in this time.

He stroked his full beard. It wasn't in style here, but he hadn't taken time to fully research the latest fads. The last coven meeting on Hedel had thrown him off-guard. He hadn't expected the plea that the gods return to Earth, help eliminate the demons that swarmed the planet, and work to bring peace to the people that they'd seeded here millennia ago.

He'd been on Earth before. Once he'd been worshipped, statues erected in his praise, women begging for him and men wishing they were he. But that had been another time, and he had no false pretenses of it happening again.

Humans had mocked his abilities, refused what he could offer. They'd turned their back on him. Religious leaders had forbidden him to enter their towns, had told him not to come around their womenfolk until in disgust, he'd left Earth.

When the goddess Bridget had sought all the gods and goddesses out, requested the coven meet, and then put in her plea for help, he'd been inclined to turn and leave quietly.

"Earth didn't care for the likes of me," he'd muttered.

But he'd been overheard. Others had complained as well, he'd sensed their discomfort in returning to the planet that no longer believed they existed. Bridget had a way about her. And she was a good goddess, unlike some of them.

There was no harm in checking the place out, seeing how it had changed since he'd left. So what if the place was overrun with demons. The nasty creatures wouldn't bother him. They only plagued the humans. And from what he'd heard of Earth over the past thousand years or so, they deserved it.

He started walking down the narrow concrete sidewalk toward the woman he'd sensed when he first arrived here. Although she was mortal, Thena Cooke as she called herself had worked hard to develop what most humans ignored. Her powers were stronger than a human's powers should be. That intrigued him. And he wouldn't deny that her smooth caramel skin, the way she held herself and moved with such grace, and her shapely figure, which her loose-fitting clothes didn't complement, had caught more than his eye's attention.

He knew she'd noticed him. Her current mishap distracted her. But she had the strength to feel him. Priapus respected that quality in her. He meant her no harm. He'd never wished harm on any human. They just hadn't wanted him around. Jealous of what he had, the men on this planet had scorned him, convincing their women to do the same.

The moist night air hung heavily around him while he watched her get out of her car. Tall and slender, her legs thin, her breasts ripe and full, her waist narrow, she moved silently across her yard, reaching to pick up her newspaper, and then headed toward her house.

He left his body standing there in the middle of the block, his spirit gliding through the darkness toward her while she worked to unlock her front door. When she looked over her shoulder, he moved closer, wanting to see her face. She looked right at him, her dark eyes staring at his soul, sensing him.

Her brow creased, while she looked down, relying on her inner eye to see him. Long thick eyelashes fluttered down over her eyes. Her eyebrows were long and thin, nicely arched, accentuating her high cheekbones and narrow face. Straight black hair pulled back into a bun allowed him to see the narrow arch of her neck. He wondered if she would shudder, let out a breath, if he were to place a kiss at her nape.

She was stunning, absolutely beautiful, her skin dark like rich milk chocolate. Even though his presence worried her, confused her, it also made her curious. She wanted to know who he was, and why he was here.

Moving backwards, sinking back into his body, he took a few steps toward her home, watching while she turned and opened the door to her home.

Priapus scratched his beard, the damn thing itching. It had been so long since he'd taken human form, walked on the streets of this planet. So much had changed. Tidy yards yielded no gardens. The houses were close together, and similar, as if no one dared to stand out. He'd heard how populated the planet had become, how they communicated with each other around the planet now. They had become scientific on Earth, having no time for worship, or for gods.

Thena shut the door behind her. The urge to open it again and march out there and demand whose powers she felt, overwhelmed her.

"You just lost your damn job," she muttered, messing her hair up when she ran her fingernails through it. "This is the last thing you need to be thinking about. Let that power go."

Staring at her dark living room, she didn't move for a minute, trying again to reach out with her mind and feel the air around her. Whoever it was, they weren't in her house.

Dropping her bag on the couch, she moved through the dark rooms to her kitchen, opening the drawer where she kept her candles and her athame, her ritual knife. She pulled out a few blue candles, already in small glass holders. Lavender would help her after the night she had. And a hot bath.

"I just can't believe after eleven years working for Benn Plastics that I'm just out the door."

She gathered her bag of lavender and her candles and headed toward her bathroom. Soaking in lavender was the best way to calm herself, get rid of the negative energy she'd allowed to fill her. Too much anger and resentment clogged her senses. A hot bath and the powers of lavender would help soothe her.

Leaving the bath to fill, she removed her work clothes, and then stared at herself in her mirror while securing the pins in her hair.

"The powers that be, protect me," she whispered, running her hands over her hair and then down her naked body. "I stand before you in my purest form. Blessed be the Gods and Goddesses."

Taking her ceremonial bowl, a simple ceramic piece her grandmother had given her as a child, she poured the dried lavender petals into it and then sprinkled them over the water. She watched the steam slowly rise as the hot water filled her tub.

Quickly, the soothing aromas of the dried plant filled her bathroom. Their energy caressed her soul, easing her mind and helping her anger to dissipate. Opening her medicine cabinet, she pulled out her matches and lit the candles on the back of her toilet.

In spite of the rich aromatic smells sifting through her bathroom, something else moved in around her as well.

The power had returned. Well, if he wanted to approach her, there wasn't a damn thing she could do about it. There was no evil, no ill feelings surrounding his power. Nonetheless, such raw strength unnerved her. She stepped into the hot water, feeling the power of the lavender tingle against her skin.

"Oh light of the moon, wrap around me, protect me, keep me from harm." She knelt into the water, cupping her hands and pouring the powers that filled her tub over her body. "Lavender you caress me, soothe me, bring light to a soul that has darkened."

A warm breeze brushed over her skin, barely touching her, but alerting her senses, bringing her nipples to hardened peaks, and at the same time sending a shiver straight to her toes. She couldn't match the power that rushed through her.

Sinking deeper into the water, she searched with her mind to find the source of the power that had joined her. No matter how hard she focused, she didn't find anyone in her home in any of her rooms. And she was ruining the pleasure of her hot bath by dwelling on it. She sank deeper into the scented water, focusing on the strength of the small lavender plant that had been used for centuries to help soothe frazzled nerves.

Closing her eyes, she ran her hands over her body, letting the water trace paths over her breasts, her thighs and legs. It soothed her body, cleansed her soul, allowed her the peace that she needed so that she could think clearly, figure out what her next path in life would be.

When she reached the moment of pure relaxation, the hot water covering her up to her neck, a sensation rippled through her that she was being watched. Again there was no evil, no threat, almost more like a curiosity, amusement.

Whoever claimed this power, seemed to understand her need to relax, to allow the tension from being fired to fade away from her. Thena knew lavender had strong powers, but it wasn't strong enough to make her feel so relaxed, so at peace with the world. The owner of the power had compassion, felt for her plight, and wished to ease her tension by helping the lavender along.

How thoughtful.

Lazily she opened an eye, running her hands over her body underneath the water. She felt arousal too. Whoever was part of this power enjoyed the view of her that they had.

"If you dare to approach me, then let yourself be known." She glanced around her empty bathroom, then at the door, which was all but closed. Barely an inch of space allowed her to see beyond into her dark bedroom.

Her heart raced, but she didn't fear the unknown. As long as she could remember, her mother and Gramma had always told her that harm came only to those who feared what they didn't know.

Something explored her, making her heart flutter, her breath quicken, her mouth go dry as she gasped for breath. She could feel the brush of power, like an intense energy pressing through the air penetrating her skin. A swarm of emotions—excitement, misery, and incredible loneliness—filled her to the point where she couldn't move.

Who are you? There was no way she could speak. Thinking as loud as she could, her body floated in the water, slowly rising until she was no longer submerged in the steamy wet heat.

She opened her eyes quickly when suddenly her front door opened. Someone had just entered her home.

She sunk to the bottom of the bathwater, splashing a fair bit of it out of the tub. Nervous energy tingled through her as she struggled to stand. She didn't hear anyone moving through her home, but someone was here. It was more than the energy that had surrounded her before. A person was in her home.

Water splattered on her bathroom tiles as she stepped out of the tub, grabbing the towel. Her wet feet left a trail on her wooden floor. She walked through her dark bedroom, sucking in a breath. The man's presence greeted her before she saw him.

Chapter Two

"You didn't need to get out of the bath for me." Priapus closed the door behind him, staring at her, her skin moist with nothing more than a towel covering her.

His cock throbbed to life at the sight of her. Long and slender, her dark skin glowing in the dim candlelight. Her ripe breasts were full, the soft flesh pushed upward above the towel.

Suddenly the clothes he wore seemed burdensome. Heat swarmed through him like a fever, erupting to life. Something primitive ignited deep inside him, building, creating an ache that pulsed through him until his cock held the brunt of it, hard and ready.

Thena looked at him, wide-eyed, while her breath came heavily, making her breasts rise and fall before him.

"Who in the hell are you?" Her voice shook and he could hear the rapid thump of her heart racing too fast, proving the effect he had on her.

"I assure you, I have nothing to do with hell." It amazed him, the amount of power he felt radiating from her.

But what captivated him even more was how incredibly beautiful she was. Dark brown eyes filled with intelligence and curiosity gave him the once-over. His body hardened as her gaze traveled down him and back up again. Her full lips were dark, like a midnight rose, and barely parted while her breath brushed over them. Once again he was captivated by her long slender neck.

The towel she wrapped around her stopped just as her long slim legs began. And her bare feet, narrow and perfectly shaped, had dark polish carefully applied to each toenail. He took her in, the fresh scent of lavender adding to her intoxicating beauty. Returning his attention to her face, he fought the urge to make the towel she grasped disappear.

"Who are you?" she asked again. One thing she sensed instantly, he was the source of the power that had approached her in the parking lot, and wrapped around her in her bathroom.

"That towel barely does you justice." A hint of a smile lit his eyes.

Thena gripped the towel, feeling him pulling at it with his mind. "Powers that be, stay away from me. Powers that be, stay away from me. Powers that be, stay away from me. So mote it be."

She watched him warily.

"Now answer my question." She should just throw him out, try one of her stronger spells to send him sliding out the door on his rear.

No matter how powerful he was, he was out of line for entering her home without a proper introduction. He'd ruined the power of her lavender, although she had to admit the anger at being fired had left her. But at the moment, that wasn't the point. If she had half a mind, she'd send him right out that door.

Something about him was different though, something that made her hesitate. And it had nothing to do with his intent gaze, the rather large size of his frame.

Power radiated from him, raw, in its purest form. She'd spent a lifetime among witches and wizards, and sorcerers. No one she'd ever met came close to bearing the strength she felt coming from the man who'd just sauntered into her home. And although she knew she should be pissed, he intrigued her.

"You called for me. I wouldn't have just barged in if you hadn't. I do have manners." He knew he didn't answer her question, give her his name.

But he was surprised to feel her energy leave her, wrap around him, confine his powers. They were weak, like being confined by thin paper, but not as weak as he'd expected a witch's powers to be. In fact, he'd never known a witch who could touch him. She not only touched him, she stopped his thoughts.

He tried searching hers, needing to know how well she knew her history, what gods she prayed to. What he pulled from her was curiosity, fascination. Her lack of fear, and her sultry body wrapped in nothing more than a towel, distracted him. He struggled to come up with a suitable name that would satisfy her.

It didn't help that he'd hovered over her bathtub, aching to pull her into his arms. He'd already seen what she had to offer. Her full round breasts, and the smooth skin that dipped down between her legs made it real hard for him to think clearly enough to come up with a name to give her. Blood pumped quickly to his large cock, and if he allowed it to harden too much, she might lose her confidence. He adjusted the long coat around him.

"I called for no one. I've done a simple incantation here and you storm in on it. And if you had manners, you would have knocked." The way he was looking at her made her tummy do little flip-flops. Nerves spilled over each other throughout her, making her shaky, her knees grow weak.

No one had ever entered her home before like this. With the amount of power emanating from him, she knew she had little to offer him. He wasn't seeking out the village witch. Although the way he looked at her, she guessed he'd seen something he liked. That thought caused her heart to race in her chest. There was no way to tell the extent of his powers. But anyone who could pull her toward him the way he had, allow her to feel his powers wrap around her, was pretty damn strong.

"You said, 'if you dare to approach me, then let yourself be known'."

"Oh my gods!" Thena stumbled backward, almost losing grip on her towel.

She'd suspected his presence in the bathroom with her. But to be strong enough to be with her, hear what she'd said, and then moments later walk through her front door. What was this man?

Priapus moved quickly. Grabbing her arm, he stabilized her, while she looked up at him with large brown eyes, beautiful sultry eyes, that at the moment showed confused astonishment.

"It's okay," he murmured, willing her to calm down.

The moment he touched her he sensed her strength. She was truly a witch. Not one of those old hags who claimed to control the elements, cast spells for a coin and rob all around them. No. Not at all. Thena was the real thing. In fact, there was untapped power hovering around her like a loving shadow. He wondered why she hadn't attempted to harness it.

There was nothing more embarrassing than being in a stranger's grasp with nothing more than a towel on. Thena couldn't catch her breath. He was the power she'd sensed at the factory and when she'd arrived home. His hand branded her skin, sending heat rushing through her so fast she couldn't get her bearings for a second. She swallowed her embarrassment, knowing if she didn't, he would best her and she'd be at his mercy.

And she had no idea what he wanted. One thing she did know, with such strong magic, anything he wanted he could have. That in itself should justify her being scared. It didn't though. Such power fascinated her. And it was controlled, strong, nothing like anything she'd ever sensed before. Tingles rushed through her, like goose bumps. Suddenly her breath came harder while her mind imagined what he might want.

His hair was long, like someone who'd been living on the streets and didn't have a way to shower or care for it regularly. A full beard covered most of his face, and hung past his chin. The coat he wore hung almost to the floor, giving her no indication of what his body looked like other than the fact that he was tall, with broad shoulders. But his eyes, a soft green, glowed with passion while he kept his gaze locked to hers, as if he could see into her deepest thoughts, and enjoyed what he saw.

"Maybe if I undressed too, you would be more comfortable," he said, reaching for the lapel of his coat.

"No. You should leave," she said quickly, taking another step backward, gripping her towel with her fist while pointing at him with her other hand. *Take your hand off of your coat*, she thought to herself, working to move her energy toward him.

"You don't want me to leave." His gaze lowered to her hand, and he reached out, touching her fingers with his own.

Energy rushed through her when his fingertips grazed over hers, fiery hot, sending a flush through her that almost made her faint. No one she'd ever met had ever touched her like that, and with a mere brushing of flesh, fingertips caressing fingertips. Her heart raced, heat rushing through her veins that consumed her so quickly she couldn't think straight. She yanked her hand back, still feeling his strength even though she no longer touched him.

"Don't tell me what I want." She wouldn't admit that he had her curiosity so piqued that she didn't want him to leave. And she wouldn't think about the fact that someone with such internal strength might be able to sense her thoughts. She fought to clear her mind. "Leave this house. Get out, now."

He smiled. And in spite of his beard, she couldn't help notice how charming a grin he had.

"You asked me to come here, and now you want me to leave already?" He took a step closer, realizing she struggled with some success to close her mind to him. "Thena, I'm not going to hurt you."

"How do you know my name?" she barely whispered, her mouth suddenly too dry.

Terror should be gripping her, standing in front of this stranger in no more than her towel.

An excited curiosity rushed through her instead. Her insides tingled with a sexual energy she hadn't experienced in a long time. Warmth grew between her legs. Her body charged with an ache to reach out and touch him, feel the raw power again that she'd experienced from the brush of his fingertips, from the touch of his hand. Underneath all of that hair, she imagined a sexy god, raw and untamed, confident and all-knowing—the man of any woman's dreams.

What the hell was she thinking? He was a complete stranger, and he'd just sauntered into her house in the middle of the night. This wasn't a dream, it was a damned nightmare.

"Tell me how you know that I'm so powerful?" he retorted, amazed at her strength given she was just a local witch.

Most village witches couldn't sense that he was a god. Some had realized he was powerful, but they had assumed, with their limited abilities, that he was another witch. Thena Cooke saw him for what he was, and now she worked to understand what she saw. There was power riveting through her that excited him, and he ached to learn more about her.

"I don't know you. But if you were a gentleman you wouldn't have barged into my home." Thena stormed out of her living room.

She grabbed her clothes, struggling to get her shirt on before he was too close again. He could sense her outrage fighting with her arousal.

"I want you out. Get out now. Get the fuck out of my house," she yelled at him, the moment she had her shirt pulled over her head.

He was inside her head, probing her senses. She didn't like not being in control.

"You are letting your human fears consume you, Thena." He helped her with her shirt, untangling it around her shoulders so that it would fall over her. But he couldn't let her go. Taking her in his arms, he pulled her to him, feeling her breasts mash against his chest while he cupped his hands over her ass. "You have such untamed power. Relax. Calm down. See that there is nothing to fear here."

Thena shoved hard against him. She pointed toward her living room. "How dare you tell me to calm down! Get the hell out of here before I call the police."

He took her arm, holding it gently in his hand, and bent over to place a kiss on the inside of her elbow. Shivers rushed through her, his beard tickling her skin, sending a rush of desire so intense through her that she gasped.

He knew her name. He knew she was a witch. This was too much. Too damned much. Everything she'd been taught. All the lessons she'd heard again and again on being discreet, on serving those who needed her but never crossing the line and bragging about her heritage, tumbled through her. A complete stranger had strolled through her front door. He knew too much about her, and she knew nothing about him, and he was seducing her, torturing her senses with his words and actions and she didn't have a fucking clue what to do about it.

There was one thing she did know. No stranger would ever seduce her. Not when she was drunk. Not when she was sober. Not in a bar or in her home. She had too much respect for her body, her soul, her own integrity.

She glared at him, gathering all of her strength, sobering her unexplained desires for this man with her anger. "I'll let you walk out of this house. But if you don't leave right now, I will force you out."

Priapus raised an eyebrow, amused.

Returning to the living room, he turned at the front door in time to see her struggling into her pants, watching him as she hobbled while pulling them up and fastening them.

"This planet hasn't changed a bit," he said, frustration pouring from him. "I didn't want to come here in the first place. But I'll be damned if I'm cast out again."

Opening her door, he disappeared into the night, not bothering to close it behind him.

Thena walked to her door and looked out into her front yard. She didn't see him out front. Even after she had stepped outside, he wasn't on the sidewalk, there was no car heading down her street.

Something funny passed through her, the oddest sensation that she'd just missed something.

Chapter Three

Over the next few days Thena did her best to adjust to normal sleeping hours. It wasn't easy after working through the nights for so many years. Waking up with the sun shining through her windows annoyed her, and the excited chatter on the morning news and radio didn't help manners.

She stood staring at her coffeepot, willing it to drip faster, when her phone rang. It didn't take magic to know who called her. Her mom had called every few hours for the past couple days. And in spite of how much she knew her mama loved her and cared about her, Thena knew her answer would be the same as it had been during the past twenty calls.

"Hi, Mom," she said, closing her eyes and envisioning her mom on the other end of the line, her long cotton gown covering her bony figure, and her silver hair coiled around the top of her head.

"Athena Lotus Cooke. How many times did I teach you that assuming something was a sign of weakness and laziness?" Her grandmother's scratchy voice sounded stern even several states away. "That big-city living is clogging your brain. When you coming home?"

Thena shook her head, it having been a long time since she'd been scolded with the use of her full name. She smiled in spite of the lack of coffee in her system.

"Hi, Gramma," she said, slurring her grandmother's name just how she did as a child. "How are you?"

"Don't you play sweet with me, missy." Her grandmother's voice faded in and out over the phone, and Thena imagined her pulling the receiver away from her face so she could glare at it. "You're needed here. Now you get your behind home straight away, before I take a stick to you. I'll be serving you at breakfast, or cursing you at dusk."

Her grandmother hung up and Thena put the receiver down on its cradle. "Well, hell," she sighed, turning her attention once again to the coffeepot.

There was no way she could think before coffee. Taking her mug, she quickly poured herself a cup of the fresh brew and then put the pot back so the remainder of the batch could drip. She turned to the phone, knowing it would ring. On half a ring, she picked it up and answered.

"Hi, Mom," she said again, knowing this time she was right.

"What did Gramma Cooke say?" Her mother sounded worried and agitated.

It didn't surprise her a bit that her mother knew that her grandmother had just called. The link between generations had always been strong.

"I'm supposed to be there by breakfast," she said. "Which is impossible," she added quickly. "You've got to help me make Gramma see that my life is here in Kansas City."

Margaret Cooke laughed, the sound pure and refreshing, so like her mother. "It would be easier to move Kansas City next to Kentucky." But then her tone turned serious. "Have you found a new job?"

Thena hadn't been looking that seriously. Something seemed to be stopping her every time she picked up the classified section of the paper. She'd even tried blessing the newspaper with sage, but no matter her efforts, the second she reached the classifieds there would be something that would distract her. If was as if strange magic prevented her from searching for work.

"Not yet," she admitted, unwilling to let her mother know the truth.

"Well, if you need money for the plane ticket, we'll come up with it. But you need to be down here. Unless you got a man calling your name, your home is here."

Thena's thoughts strayed to the stranger who had so boldly entered her home the other night. She hadn't seen him anywhere since, except in her thoughts. And he seemed to be lingering there on a regular basis, driving her crazy. Memories of his fingers stroking her skin still drove her nuts. The way he'd touched her, gazed down on her with those soft green eyes, had distracted her more than she would admit.

"Mom, do you really think I would find decent work down there?" She hadn't been back to Kentucky in years. Thanks to the Internet, and free long distance, she kept in touch with her mom on a weekly basis. But Kansas City was her home now.

"There is plenty of work here for you to do." Margaret applied that quiet tone, the one she only used when she was making a point that those who didn't have *the gift* wouldn't understand. "Thena. I need your help."

Margaret Cooke never asked for anyone's help. An uncomfortable feeling settled in Thena's gut, the sensation that something was terribly wrong. She slid the spaghetti strap of her dress back up her narrow shoulder, wrinkling her brow as she squinted at the morning sun through her kitchen window.

"What's wrong, Mom?"

"You'll see when you get here. Things aren't right. It's time to come home."

Thena hung up the phone with an unsettling feeling sinking in her tummy. Her mom had been vague, but it wasn't Margaret Cooke's nature to complain unless something was terribly out of sorts.

Sipping at her coffee, she wondered what had her mother so worried. With years of practice and meditating, Thena had mastered sensing other's thoughts when they were around her. But try as she did, she couldn't reach across the states, detect what might be amiss so far away.

And she knew she wouldn't be satisfied until she found out what her mother had meant. Staring at the pen lying on her table, she made it roll back and forth with her mind, a simple act she'd mastered as a child. Her thoughts drifted though, giving little thought to the pen moving.

Once again the man who'd entered her home appeared in her thoughts, unbeckoned. She reached out with her mind, searching. No matter where she searched, there were no powers anywhere near by, let alone someone who possessed the strength she'd sensed in him.

That was the one thing she'd never liked about Kansas City. At least at home, when she reached out with her thoughts, there was her mom and her grandmother. No matter how many covens she'd sought out here, she'd never felt that same bonding that she'd had with her own kin.

"Well, hell." She really didn't want to go down to Kentucky. It had been high school the last time she'd been home, and she didn't miss the place a bit.

She'd left her home, searching out a new life, when she'd grown tired of being persecuted, taunted, belittled, because she was different from everyone else. Just because she came from a family of witches didn't make her a bad person.

"And if I leave here, would it be because I'm running once again?" She scratched her fingernails through her short, straightened hair.

Maybe she was using the excuse that her mom was worried about something as the reason to leave. And in truth, her humiliation at being fired and not being appreciated for what she was made it easy to leave town, to once again run away.

If anyone were to approach her, ask her how to best handle a problem such as this, she would commend them for talking about it, encourage them to meditate, seek out the gods for consolation and advice.

"Think you're smart enough to take your own advice?" she grumbled as she ran her fingers over her head, straightening her hair back down so that it pressed smoothly against her head, stopping at the nape of her neck. Standing and stretching, she felt the tension in the air, the past few days of being home and pondering her situation having clogged the energy in her home. The least she could do was burn some sage, clean house, and her mind. Then maybe a knowledge spell, or a searching incantation would help.

Thena had been raised to approach the gods in a proper manner. One didn't go seeking help dressed in rags and not clean. Showing respect, and presenting oneself looking your best, was plain and simple good manners.

Entering her bathroom off of her bedroom, she applied some of her hair gel, greasing her short hair back until it was smooth and shiny, glistening black against the light. She chose her long hairpiece, fixing it to the back of her head with her pins, and then carefully applied makeup. After wrapping a red scarf around her hair, putting it up in a ponytail, Thena padded through her bedroom, the wooden floor under her feet cool against her skin. She stripped out of the simple sundress she'd put on that morning, and then took a deep breath, again distracted by what had happened a few days ago when she'd been caught naked in her home by a stranger.

"The best thing to do when you fall off a bike is to get right back on," she told herself firmly, knowing if she kept her clothes on, she would be surrendering to her preoccupation that she might be interrupted again.

Most everything she needed to perform the simple incantation of seeking advice was on her dresser—her oils and candles, and a wooden incense holder with fresh sage lying in it.

Tradition stated the chant should be done before a full moon, but she didn't want to wait for nightfall to seek out the gods. "And there's nothing wrong with compromise," she said out loud while turning on her lamp and then wrapping one of her scarves around the lampshade to focus the light.

Taking the plate her oils sat on, she poured one of her oils on it in a circle, sprinkled some of the sage over it, and then lit it on fire. She positioned the light so that it shone in the middle of the burning circle, and then began her chant.

Her athame was a small dagger, no bigger than her hand. Its wooden handle was worn smooth from the many times she'd used it. Having been a gift from her grandmother when she'd turned sixteen, she'd never replaced it.

Holding it now, she used it to draw a mental line through the air.

"I call to the east, to the rising sun." She turned, raising her arms while she cleared her thoughts and allowed her soul to open to her spell. She continued. "To the south with its warmth, to the west, where the sun sleeps, to the north, with its cool refreshing air."

Cutting the air with the athame, she created a circle around herself.

Thena turned to the small fire that burned on the plate on her dresser. She ran her small dagger through the smoke, swaying its path. The lamplight shone over her hands, her skin glowing. "Good light. Full light. Light that shines upon me. Guide me and show me what I must know."

The words were barely uttered, yet no one needed to hear them in the conventional manner. Closing her eyes, holding her hands in the smoke, feeling the heat of the fire, the herbs filling her with their rich scent, she repeated her words.

"Ease the trouble from my mind so that I may see what troubles my family." She let her head fall back, feeling the powers of her spell consume her, images dancing through a fog in her mind.

Darkness consumed her, shadows moving just beyond her mind's eye that she couldn't focus on.

Something was wrong. There was trouble. Things weren't as they appeared. None of it made any sense.

"Things aren't right." Her mother's words echoed through her head.

Her phone rang and she ignored it, swaying slightly while she struggled to figure out what she saw in her mind. Nothing would come into focus though. The strangest sensation that she was seeing people she knew, yet they weren't who they appeared to be, taunted her. Chills rushed over her body. The fire beneath her fingers no longer burned hot, but icy cold. She shivered, closing her eyes tighter while she struggled to understand what was being shown to her.

Thena, I'm not going to hurt you. The words of the stranger who'd entered her house the other night brushed through her, whispered so close to her head that she knew if she opened her eyes he would be standing right next to her.

Her body responded to him, her nipples hardening while her breasts swelled, aching to be touched, caressed. Her tummy flip-flopped, a sudden desire warming the chill she'd felt moments before. Pressure peaked between her legs, the growing urge to be touched, stroked and fondled distracting her.

"Guide me and show me what I must know." She had to concentrate, allow her magic to guide her.

The sage burned rich around her, cleaning the cobwebs from her brain. She focused on it, doing her best to push out all other thoughts while imagining the sage moving through her home, ridding it of the frustration and animosity she'd experienced over the past few days.

The rooms of her house faded from her mind all too quickly though.

Darkness continued to envelop her, images walking around her, just out of her line of vision so that she couldn't see them. And they didn't want to be seen. That realization bothered her. People, or creatures, or something, lingered just out of range of her vision, hiding, whispering among themselves. They knew she watched them and they didn't like it. Uneasiness sank in her gut. No one intentionally hid unless they were up to no good.

Then there were faces, familiar and almost forgotten. The people she'd grown up with, members of her hometown. They moved, walked past her, there but not there. It was as if something had consumed them, made them appear normal but something wasn't right.

A hard knock on her door startled her, sending the images flying from her mind.

"Shit," Thena gasped, falling backwards, losing her spell. Grabbing the side of her bed, she managed to not fall on her rear. "Damn it."

Quickly she blew out the small fire burning on the plate and then grabbed her dress, struggling to pull it over her head as whoever it was knocked again even louder.

"Thena. Let me in." It was her friend Naomi. "You better open this door before Merco forces it open."

The concern in her friend's voice made Thena hurry, and she quickly adjusted her dress over her before flipping the lock and opening the door to her friends' concerned faces.

"I tried to call," Naomi said, her smile apologetic.

"I'm sorry. I was busy." Thena ran her hands down her dress, her thoughts still filled with the images she'd seen while working her magic.

She backed up to let her friends in. Naomi had been her friend for years, the two of them having worked at the factory together. Naomi had left the factory, and married Merco, a man Thena didn't know well, but who seemed nice enough. One thing she did know about him from the few times she'd met him before, he possessed a level of magic, of power, that surpassed her own. The few times she'd approached the subject with Naomi, her friend had quickly changed the subject. Thena had interpreted that as her friend wanting to keep the matter private.

"We were worried about you." Naomi immediately made herself comfortable, sitting on the edge of Thena's couch. "Merco thought we should come check on you. How are you doing?"

Thena smiled, trying to appear relaxed. "Still licking my wounds over being fired."

Naomi frowned and nodded. "They were stupid to fire you."

Thena glanced at Merco, a tall man with dark features and quite good-looking. His expression wasn't readable but she felt his gaze probing her, and suddenly the intense power she'd experienced the other night in the parking lot of the factory, and then again when the stranger had entered her home, filled the room.

She sucked in a breath, trying her best to hide her sudden surprise. Whatever she felt was strong, overwhelming, powers so intense there was nothing to compare them with. She'd only been around Merco a few times, and although she'd sensed his magical strength in the past, for some reason now it seemed to saturate through her, making it hard to concentrate. It didn't make any sense. His powers seemed to be as strong as what she'd sensed from the stranger the other day.

"What's done is done," she mumbled, turning so that she wasn't looking at either of them. "There is a reason why I don't have my job any longer and now I just have to figure out what that is."

Maybe her spell still lingered around her, clouding her perception. That had been known to happen before, her magic making it difficult for her to see what was in front of her while her thoughts still dwelt on images that were no longer there. There was no way Merco and that stranger could both be so powerful. But what she felt, what coursed through her was magic strong enough to fill the room, steal her breath, make it hard to think straight.

"Merco was just saying on the way over here that you should take advantage of not working right now, visit family…"

Thena turned and stared at her friend, then at Merco. She licked her lips, thinking maybe she was being given the answer to her spell through her friends. Merco moved to stand behind Naomi, placing his hand possessively on her shoulder. He didn't say anything but his attention was focused on Thena. She glanced at him only for a moment then lowered her gaze to Naomi's concerned look.

"My mom did call me this morning." And the day before, but Thena didn't want to go into details about how her family worried over her. "She asked me to come down there."

"Good. Then it's settled. We can give you a ride to the airport if you need it," Merco said, and then ran his hand down Naomi's arm. "We have errands to run. But Thena, you'll call if you need anything."

Naomi stood, and then gave Thena a quick hug before returning to Merco's side. He didn't smile, but his expression was relaxed, friendly in a serious sort of way. But that wasn't what grabbed Thena's attention. She respected power, and knew Merco was strong. But the way he'd seemed to already know that Thena needed to leave town made her realize that was why they'd stopped by.

Well, at least now she had a ride to the airport.

By the end of the day, she had plane tickets, and had arranged for Naomi to keep an eye on her place. Packing lightly, she climbed into the backseat of Naomi and Merco's car when they arrived to pick her up, and headed out toward the airport.

After dealing with security and getting her boarding pass, she moved slowly with the flow of people through the tunnel-like hallway onto the waiting plane that would take her back to Kentucky, to the place where she'd been born and raised, to the home she hadn't seen since she left for the city right after high school.

The plane was cramped, and it seemed like the line of people who moved past her would never end once she'd found her seat and put her small bag in the overhead compartment.

A man, dressed like so many others on the plane, approached her. He wore a gray pinstripe suit, professional-looking, with striking good looks. He moved patiently, waiting while those in front of him found their assigned seats. When he glanced toward her, soft green eyes captured her gaze, a power so strong imprisoning her while she stared back at him.

It was the man who'd entered her home the other night!

Shit! Thena stared, unable to believe the transformation. Gone was the beard, the long trench coat, the attire of a street person. Clean-cut, with short brown hair, the man moved closer until he hovered over her, never looking away.

Thena's mouth went dry. She stared up at him in disbelief. He stopped next to her, looking down, his soft green eyes seeming to see her deepest thoughts. Her insides did a little flip-flop. Sudden warmth surrounded her as if he'd just pulled her into his arms. The throbbing of her heart matched the pulse that started between her legs.

Don't fear me. He didn't move his mouth, but she heard him speak to her plain as day.

He passed on by, moving with the rest of the people down the narrow aisle, and Thena turned to watch him. No matter that his back was to her now, she would swear he hovered right by her. If she closed her eyes, she would feel him touching her, holding her like a child, offering protection so strong and secure she had nothing to compare to it. But she couldn't close her eyes. There was no way she could take her gaze from him. Finally he disappeared when he sat down quite a ways toward the back of the plane.

Thena's tummy balled into knots of anticipation. And it had nothing to do with the plane taking off.

Chapter Four

From what Priapus knew about airplanes, this wasn't the best that Earth had to offer. The long, narrow compartment was cramped, the seats close together, and people packed in like some of the slave ships he'd seen in other galaxies. Yet these people climbed aboard of their own will, the conversations he overheard making it clear most were excited to be traveling, or anxious to return home.

Over the past few days, he'd wandered the planet, bringing himself up to date with the times. In essence, not much had changed here. They were more modern, advancing like most civilizations did on planets. The gods had been forgotten, these people no longer caring where they'd come from, or how they got here.

He saw why Bridget had appealed to the coven. This place was a prime candidate for evil to lurk. Humans here on Earth were so busy trying to advance themselves, they wouldn't look twice at a demon if it bit them in the ass.

Word had traveled that the leader of the demons no longer existed, that several of the gods had managed to end his torturous life. He'd taken the knowledge lightly, having never given the demons too much thought.

"The demons are struggling to take over Earth." Bridget's words from the last coven meeting came back to him. "And without a leader, they've divided into sections, each of them growing stronger since the humans don't fight them off."

Almost two thousand Earth years had passed since he'd been to this planet. The place no longer interested him and he'd barely paid attention during the coven meeting. Yet somehow the information had bothered him. Demons couldn't be allowed to take over Earth. No matter that the people on this planet had turned their backs on him. If they gained this planet, they would move on to the next, growing stronger, and that couldn't be allowed. Better to keep them in the hells where they belonged.

He'd sensed Thena's strength shortly after arriving here. And one thing he learned over the past few days, there weren't many humans like her. She was strong, her magic unusually strong for a human. Most people on Earth didn't use the sense they'd been given, let alone work to develop the part of them that would aid them in working the elements, make the best out of the lives that they'd been given.

And he still wasn't convinced he cared to help them. They'd shunned him. In his natural human form, they'd turned their backs on what he had to offer and made fun of him.

Something about Thena was different than the other humans. She intrigued him. And that was saying something since most people he'd interacted with since arriving here had bored him to death.

He lingered at the back of the plane, having made sure that Thena was safe. He had no desire to stay aboard however, and could easily keep an eye on her until she landed. Opening the door to the tiny bathroom, he disappeared before the door closed on him.

Thena remained sitting when the other passengers shuffled off after the plane landed. She watched everyone pass by her, waiting to see the stranger again.

"Is everything okay, ma'am?" a stewardess asked, when she was clearly the last person on the plane. The woman's expression was polite but it was obvious she was anxious for Thena to gather her things and leave.

"Yes. Fine." She stood, glancing behind her, sure she hadn't missed him, yet he was obviously no longer on the plane.

That was strange. And she didn't like the pang of disappointment that rushed through her as she snatched the only bag she'd brought with her. He wouldn't have walked past her without her noticing. His powers were too strong. She hadn't seen him though.

But what did it matter if she had missed him?

Frustrated with her torn feelings, she entered the busy airport, glad that she'd packed light and didn't need to mess with retrieving bags.

"Baby! My baby!" Margaret Cooke yelled loud enough to turn heads, not that her bright red dress with matching turban wouldn't do the trick.

"Mom." Thena grinned from ear to ear, giving her mom a warm embrace in the middle of the crowded terminal.

Her mom was thinner than she remembered her being, and smaller. She wrapped her arms around her mother's petite frame, feeling her bones. The thought that her mother was getting old, her body not as strong as it once was, made her ease up and look down into her mother's glowing face. Her mom looked pleased as punch.

"Now why are you all upset about things?" It was so like her mother to sense her emotions. Margaret's soft tone, a husky voice that caressed the air as she spoke, matched the soft brown eyes that studied Thena. "Just feel how you are all on edge. There ain't a thing to be worried about now. Everything's going to be just fine, you'll see. We're united once again as we should be."

No matter how long she'd been away, Thena knew that arguing with her mother would get her nowhere. She didn't feel the least bit worried. Maybe a bit preoccupied when the stranger hadn't gotten off the plane, but there was no reason to mention that.

"It's real good to see you," she whispered, giving her mother another quick hug.

"And your Gramma is waiting back at the house." Margaret held on to her as she maneuvered through the crowd of people.

There was a change in her mother's mood when she mentioned Gramma. Something like worry, resembling a dampness in the air that settled around them. Thena wondered what had her mother concerned but didn't have time to dwell on it.

Toward the exit she saw him. Leaning against the wall, near one of the fast-food restaurants, the stranger stood watching her. Those soft green eyes penetrated right through her, stealing her breath.

"What's that?" Her mom paused, looking around her. "Do you feel that?"

Thena struggled to speak, her mouth suddenly too dry. "I don't know," she managed to say, feeling foolish since she'd stopped walking and was staring right at him.

"That's enough power to be a god," her mother whispered, glancing around her.

Her mother didn't notice him though. Thena gathered that much from the way she looked around her.

"A god?" She wanted to ask her mother if there was any history of a god taking human form in recent times.

For some reason, she didn't want to point him out though. Warmth spread through her, his gaze seeming to pull her in. If she let her mother know he stood right there, she would have to justify the strange attraction she felt to him. And right now, she couldn't explain that to herself, let alone her mother.

Who are you? It wasn't the first time she'd asked him, and even in her thoughts, asking him without speaking, she wondered why he kept that information from her.

The answer didn't come from his mouth. It was as if what she wanted to know lingered around him, hanging in the air, and she had to reach out and grab it.

Priapus. My name is Priapus.

"What is this going on here?" Her mother stopped, her hands on her hips while she looked around her, and then at Thena. "This isn't magic. This is stronger than magic."

Her tone had filled with concern. Her mom's gaze made her uncomfortable.

"I don't know, Mom. I really don't know."

It amazed Thena how Margaret Cooke, who dripping wet couldn't possibly weigh more than ninety pounds, suddenly had the strength to grab her by the arm, and almost drag her out of the terminal.

Once out of the airport traffic and headed south in her mom's car, Thena tried to relax for her mother's sake. The woman could sense her emotions as if she were chattering out loud. And Thena didn't want her mother worrying because a complete stranger, who had the strength of a god, preoccupied her thoughts. Instead she tried conjuring up her hometown, remembering the folks she'd grown up with, wondering how many of them were still around.

"Not much changes in Barren. You'll see." Her mother's habit of answering her thoughts hadn't changed any. "We got a few new restaurants, although I can't say I been to none of them. We've got our friends and our enemies, just as it's always been."

"You said there was trouble," Thena prompted, and instantly sensed her mother's emotions change.

Something dark swarmed around her. Worry. Fear. Thena couldn't label it. But she didn't like the feeling that rushed through her and that suddenly filled the car.

"You just see for yourself what you see. Then we'll figure it out together." And her mother got that pursed-lipped expression that she would always get when she wasn't going to say another word on the matter.

Thena stared out at the rolling hills, the beautiful countryside she'd always loved as a child. Kentucky sure was a piece of heaven. But her thoughts were clouded the rest of the drive. Something bothered her mother. Something unpleasant enough that she didn't want to talk about it. And Thena sensed, although she couldn't be sure, that it was something her mother couldn't handle on her own. That in itself put an uneasy knot in Thena's tummy.

Chapter Five

Priapus hovered cross-legged over the small gate that was latched shut and enclosed the Cooke property. The wooden fence wasn't painted, and the yard hadn't been kept up, unmown grass growing over old flowerbeds. But the place was clean, small and simple, yet filled with love.

He ached to talk to Thena again, touch her again. Something about her called him to her, her compelling beauty, the natural raw power that floated around her. Humans didn't usually have this effect over him. He'd learned over the centuries that most couldn't handle what he had to offer.

Yet for the past couple of days she'd been surrounded by her kinfolk. Not that she had a lot of family. From what he'd seen, her mother and grandmother were about the size of it. And the old women hovered around Thena like she was a fine piece of art that might be damaged if they let her out of their sight.

Thoughts of putting the two older women to sleep for a while, just so he could be alone with her, crossed his mind.

Thena's frustration, her confusion over what she'd found out after arriving down here, had him curious. Most humans couldn't spot a demon. And Thena didn't realize that was what she saw. But the tiny town of Barren, Kentucky, was full of them. And when he'd followed her into Bowling Green, he'd found them there too.

He'd cast a few of them out, just for old time's sake. But there was some serious housecleaning needed in these parts. From what he could tell, no other gods hovered in the area.

These people wouldn't appreciate his efforts though. He couldn't see how humans had changed that much. It would be just like it was before.

Thena stood inside the window of her mother's home. He watched her look out the window briefly, sensing him, wondering where he was, reaching out for him. Yet she didn't know him, didn't understand him. Her interest was pure curiosity, and he ached to show her more, give her more, take her interest to a new level. More than anything he wanted her to reach out to him because she wanted *him*.

His cock stirred to life in his pants, throbbing against his thigh. He wondered what she would think of him, how she'd react seeing him naked. Would she scream? Faint like ladies in the past had? Would she back off, horrified, shaking her head and then turning and running? Memories of rejection flooded through him, of women who'd flirted and teased until they'd seen the size of his cock.

The stories that made the history books that had been passed down by word of mouth, that many had chosen to believe, made him out to be the gigolo. Men would scorn him, threaten him if he didn't stay away from their womenfolk.

"They might as well fuck a donkey as take you on. You're a freak." The words had burned through him.

And in his youth he'd allowed his wrath to destroy their homes, their villages, curse them for their lack of respect.

Of course, there had been the ladies who'd lusted after him, his size having a mysterious appeal to them.

"There's not a man out there who can compare," they would whisper, in sated satisfaction. "Priapus, I will worship you always."

He shifted in the air, allowing room for his growing cock while he watched Thena move around in her mother's home. The simple white tank top she wore drew attention to her slender shoulders, her beautiful caramel-colored skin.

"It's time for the older ladies to go to sleep." He moved through the air, leaving his body hovering while his soul approached the house, passing through the walls when he knew she was alone.

No matter the women he'd been with in the past. Ancient history most of it. Even those who had adored him only kept his attention for so long. Whether goddess or mortal, none of them had captured his heart, pinned him down.

Thena pulled him in though, her slender body, the smooth nape of her neck that he longed to kiss, her long bare legs. She wore shorts that showed off the sweet curve of her ass. Even in his spiritual form, his soul ached to be one with her, feel her from the inside.

Priapus floated next to her, taking in her determined expression, the way her shirt clung to her breasts, her thin frame, and the way she glided with the beauty of a goddess.

Thena turned, the atmosphere in the room changing, knowing that some presence had appeared. Her mother's living room was quiet, the small lamp in the corner offering little more than long shadows over the simple furniture that hadn't changed since she was a child.

"Who's there?" she whispered, and then glanced quickly toward the staircase her mother and grandmother had ascended just a short while ago.

She'd just blown out the candles and their fragrances lingered around her. But something else did more than linger. Energy that was strong, with an urgency and purpose about it, moved into her space, filling her own psychic aura.

While staring at the staircase, she recognized the power of the stranger, and couldn't help but wonder if his arrival was coincidence with her mother and Gramma suddenly wanting to go to bed, and in the middle of a serious discussion, no less.

Without warning, her mother and grandmother had stood.

"It's late."

"I can't keep my eyes open another minute."

"You better have clean sheets on Thena's bed."

Thena had stood as well, hugging each of them as they turned to call it a night.

"You need to sleep soon too," her grandmother had said, her frail body pressing against Thena's for a moment with a loving embrace.

She still smelled of cinnamon and wine, the way she always had. Thena smiled down at her leathery face. "I'll go to bed real soon. I promise."

Thena studied the dark room, and then glanced again toward the stairs. More than likely they were asleep, but she wouldn't chance it if they weren't. And she was sure he was here. Slipping into her sandals, she slowly turned the front door and let herself out into the night. If the stranger were here, maybe he would show himself. She didn't want an audience if she had a chance to talk to him again.

Her heart began racing in her chest, nervous anticipation sending shivers over her warm skin. Closing the door behind her she walked through the yard. The fresh smell of cut grass lingered in the damp night air, but otherwise, the smell of herbs, of flowers growing along the path, of the newly chopped wood kept out back for the fireplace—all of those smells were gone.

Thena sighed, knowing her mom needed a fair bit of help around the place, but at the moment her thoughts were a bit distracted. The night air clung to her skin, moist and warm as she walked through the yard she'd played in as a child. So many things were different, yet still the same. Her eyes adjusted, while dew that already soaked the grass made her feet damp against her sandals.

You're out here. I can feel you. She strained to see through the darkness, the man she couldn't stop thinking about seeming all too close.

Then make me appear before you. He seemed to answer her thoughts, and her brow wrinkled as she took in the yard around her.

"Appear before me." Thena wasn't sure what to expect.

He'd just spoken in her mind. She knew that. Never before had she experienced telepathic abilities. A memory rushed through her, like a window being yanked open suddenly, allowing a view that wasn't there a moment before.

When she was a child, she'd remembered swearing she knew when the family dog was hungry, or needed to go out to the bathroom, just by looking at him. Her mother had chuckled, saying there was nothing better than seeing raw power on display.

"But I'm not a dog." Priapus appeared before her while he continued to hover over the fence.

Thena slapped her hand to her mouth, silencing a scream. "Who are you?"

He'd thought about making up a name, giving her something suitable that offered no meaning, no history, no preconceived notions. But he knew she already knew the answer, that she'd heard him in the airport. And he didn't want to insult her intelligence—more like explore it.

"Priapus," he said without ceremony, deciding at that moment he would let her make her own judgment.

"Priapus," she whispered, testing out the name.

He had told her in the airport, offered her the knowledge in her thoughts. And now he was before her, offering the same information with words.

Such an odd name. Somehow it fit him, as unusual as he was. The way he sat there, hovering in the air, he reminded her of a genie, waiting to fulfill her first wish. But he didn't look like any genie she'd ever imagined.

Envy raced through her at the ease in the way he displayed his powers. A moment hadn't passed in her life when she didn't worry that she would do something that would make someone judge her, ridicule or taunt her for being different. Yet obviously in whatever world he lived in, showing a complete stranger the strength of his magic didn't faze him in the least.

At the same time, a strange yearning, causing a flutter in her gut, a warmth to spread through her, made her want to know him better.

"Priapus," she repeated, simply staring at him.

Then it hit her. "Priapus is the god of fertility, the god who protects..."

Images of pictures she'd seen of the ancient god Priapus sprang into her mind, an uncontrollable flutter traveling through her, leaving a throbbing heat between her legs.

Her gaze lowered. "If you're Priapus, then your cock hangs halfway down your leg."

Heat tore at her cheeks in spite of her attempt at being bold. She put her hands on her hips, refusing to stand down even though embarrassment washed through her.

Priapus straightened until he stood before her, distracted by the rose flush that colored her pretty face. In the dark, her eyes glowed like onyx. The part of his body she'd just referred to stretched against his groin, encouraging his actions to be closer to her.

"History tends to distort the truth." For some reason he didn't want to boast in front of her.

But he ached to show her, to feel her hands stroking his shaft, watch that flush return to her face, although this time from lust.

"Yes it does," she managed to whisper. "And you are that Priapus?"

He stood so close to her, inhaling her sweet scent, mesmerized by her caramel skin that appeared like dark silk. The full curve of her breasts pressed against her shirt, making him itch to reach out, test their softness. When he looked at her he felt hungry—no, ravenous.

"I am the *only* Priapus." It amazed him that he could feel her powers surrounding her. "And you're more than just a witch."

"Well, thank you for that." She didn't move, knowing damn well and good that she couldn't. Her legs were like jelly and her heart raced so hard she had a hard time not panting with him standing so damned close. But she wouldn't let him taunt her. "And I am sure you aren't some ancient god."

"What makes you so sure?" His voice had gone deeper, bordering on a husky whisper.

"Because gods don't walk among us."

Priapus couldn't help but smile. "That's not what you're thinking."

"Don't tell me what I'm thinking." She scowled, looking even more adorable as her eyes darkened, challenging him.

"As you wish." Her daring turned him on, made the blood rush through him. He felt more alive than he had in centuries. "Then I'll tell you this. You are beautiful. Captivating. And I'm going to kiss you."

She barely had time to digest his words when he leaned forward and brushed his lips over hers. Just a mere touch.

The warmth of her lips, the full softness of them, burned through him with a fever so fierce it stole his breath. Glancing down at her, watching her lashes flutter over her dark orbs, he needed more. Tasting her again, sensing no resistance, he pulled at her lip.

Thena could have been floating and she wouldn't have realized it. When he pressed his mouth against hers, the intensity of his powers surged through her, filling her like a thick liqueur. She leaned her head back, unable to stop him, unwilling to let the moment pass.

With just a kiss, her insides melted. Damn it to the wind, there was no way she could make him stop. He was a stranger, a mystery. With the nonsense he talked, and the strength that emanated from him, she should be running, not leaning into him to deepen the kiss. And of all places, in her mama's yard, right outside where she could be spotted at any moment.

"Thena, give me more," he breathed, whispering into her mouth.

And all she could do was obey. What was this strange magic he placed on her?

Offering her mouth, opening up to him, she let out a sigh while her head fell back, her world spinning around her. He dipped inside her, in an enticing dance of tongues while he carefully explored her mouth.

More muscles pressed against her than she'd ever experienced in her life. He held her tight by her arms, not wrapping his arms around her, but pinning her, holding her still and close to him while he deepened the kiss. She couldn't raise her arms to pull him closer with the way he held her. It wasn't that he held her too hard. His long fingers wrapped around her arms confidently. But the strength that surged through him, and then slowly filtered through her, left her paralyzed with need.

But it was probably a damn good thing he did hold her still. The world seemed to sway to the side while she closed her eyes, allowing him to devour her mouth, feeling the heat of his body against every inch of her.

Her nipples hardened while her breasts swelled, aching against his hard chest. She managed a small step closer, pressing her hips against him and feeling his erection.

The rock-hard length of him traveled from her pelvic bone clear up past her hip. A fog surrounded her senses. She'd traveled to a place where warmth and security encompassed her, capturing her rational thought, making it impossible to focus on anything other than the tender and thorough way he kissed her. Anything could be going on around her and she was sure she wouldn't notice. The only thing she could focus on at that moment was that as the world rotated around them, they stood still, wrapped into each other, a bonding of energies making her feel more powerful than she ever had before. And with just a damn kiss.

He gripped her arms, fighting not to pull her hard against him. He wanted to feel all of her, taste all of her, devour every inch of the sultry body that leaned into him.

Her powers were stronger than he'd realized at first. He held on to her when she started floating, having given into her emotions so willingly that her magic consumed her. She didn't stop kissing him, didn't tense, and as fogged as her thoughts were he guessed she didn't realize her feet had left the ground. Her soul parted with her body, and he moved with it, keeping them together. Whether she realized the extent of their bond at that moment or not, the sultry glow of her aura was a warmth he'd never experienced before, and didn't wish to let go of.

Priapus knew the moment her thoughts came into focus. She ended the kiss, lowering her head, gasping for breath. Her body lowered against his, having left the ground a few inches and then floated down into his arms.

"What was that?" she whispered, not looking at him but focusing down, so that her black hair shone like ebony silk under the moonlight.

Something a lot stronger than a mere kiss had just passed through them. Her belly button tingled, the way it always did when she slid out of her body momentarily. But reaching that level of magic only came after serious meditation, not a kiss.

"You know the answer to that question," he told her, not wanting to let her go.

He ran his hands down her arms and took her hands in his. She wasn't petite, although she wasn't incredibly tall either. Her full breasts pressed against his chest. Her forehead reached his mouth. He brushed a kiss against her skin, willing her to raise her face to him again.

"I've prayed to the gods to come to me, help me, aid me when I needed them. I've never prayed for you." She shook her head, distracted by his cock throbbing between them.

Whoever the hell he was, if the pulsating beast between them was any indication, he was larger than any normal man should be.

"You asked me to appear before you. Thena, look at me."

And she did. She looked up into those soft green eyes and somehow knew that he wouldn't harm her, wouldn't do anything she didn't want him to do. He was strong, held more powers in his little finger probably than she could ever hope to obtain. Being this close to him made it hard to breathe, think, let alone comprehend what he might be if he weren't a god.

But she had to grab a hold of some of her sanity, keep her wits about her. If he were, in fact, a true god—and that thought was almost too much to fathom—then she wouldn't make a complete ass of herself in front of him.

"How do you know my name?" She relaxed her hands in his, dwelling for a moment on the calm strength that radiated from his touch.

"Athena Lotus Cooke. It's a perfect name for you. Named after such a brave goddess, and the beautiful water lily."

"I was born on the floor of a dirt shack. My mom says a lily is the prettiest thing that grows out of mud and water." She felt silly the second she shared the private thought with him and so stopped. There wasn't any reason for him to know the rest. She'd never been sure of the facts anyway.

"You are the beautiful water flower, blooming and glowing with elegance." He let go of her hands. Tracing paths up her arms, he ran his fingers down her slender neck. "You are my lotus blooming."

Pressing her lips together, she moved her gaze to his chest. The urge to run her fingers over his shirt, feel his muscles against her palms, brought her pause.

So he knew her name. There were ways he could find that out. "What else do you know about me?"

"I know you want me," he told her, and wrapped his arm around her, using his free hand to cup her chin, bring her mouth to his.

When she stretched into him, she became all that mattered. He spread his fingers down her neck, kissing her thoroughly and then running his tongue down her neck while he cupped her breast.

So full, so ripe, a groan escaped him while he felt the hardened peak of her nipple against his palm. Pressing his mouth to the sensitive part of her nape, it tasted as enticing as he'd anticipated. Her skin was silk, soothing a tortured soul.

Thena couldn't breathe. Powers stronger than she could imagine surged through her. If she didn't clear her head she would explode, turn to molten lava at his feet, beg him to fuck her right here and now in her mother's yard.

None of that was acceptable.

Taking a step backwards she gulped in air, refusing to look at him for a moment while she desperately tried to gather her wits about her.

Priapus' hands strayed down her body, determined to pull her back to him. "Let me—"

"No." Thena shook her head, turning away from him.

He took her arm, moving around her so that he faced her once again. He cupped her chin in his palm and she closed her eyes.

"Let me take you somewhere." A private garden he'd enjoyed during a different time came to mind, perfectly secluded.

"I'm not going anywhere with you." She moved again, and he was surprised at the defensive wall that she put up suddenly.

Not strong enough to dissolve, but stronger than he'd guessed a human would have been able to muster.

She looked up at him, knowing she needed to take control of matters quickly. He was a stranger. And relationships seldom worked for her anyway. She'd accepted a long time ago that she was different, and few could accept what she took naturally.

But what if he really is a god?

If he were a god, he wouldn't stay, but simply enter her life to help and then be on his way to help someone else. She knew her history, knew that the gods didn't settle down for a long life with a loved one. They were immortals, deities who saw to the needs of all humans. She crossed her arms over her chest, picturing a brick wall that perfectly captured her heart in a box. It was an image she'd used before to prevent herself from being hurt.

"Don't block me out, Thena." His tone changed in spite of his attempt at remaining calm. But whatever spell she'd just mentally concocted, she'd managed to tune out her thoughts, her emotions. He could no longer read her.

Humans can't block the powers of a god. What the hell is this?

"I can't allow myself to be toyed with by someone who will enter my life and then leave." The heart she'd confined in her private brick box swelled painfully. She took in a slow breath, holding her head high. "And at this point, there is nothing to block out."

"You regret kissing me?" He searched until he found the mental block she'd put up against him. It was very well-practiced, her way of keeping herself from getting hurt.

"I'm not a liar. I'm pretty sure I enjoyed it as much as you did. But it's not something I make a habit of doing. And since I don't know you, I have no idea what type of woman you are accustomed to, but I'm not one to just run off with a stranger."

And with that she turned from him, and walked back into her mother's house.

Chapter Six

Barren, Kentucky, had one grocery store, and more times than not, it took twice as long to get just a few items because it was the mandatory custom to catch up on the gossip while shopping. Some things never changed.

Thena didn't remember everyone, but vague recollections came to her as her mother patiently repeated her mantra to every curious person who approached them.

"You remember my daughter, Thena. Come all the way from Kansas City to give her mom a hand." Her proud tone never wavered.

By the time they reached the checkout, Thena was more than ready to leave and return home. Not to mention she was sick and tired of hearing how proud her mama was of her—her daughter who'd come home to be with her mother—her daughter who was, in truth, unemployed.

"Thena Cooke. Well, I'll be. When did you get back in town?" A heavy-set black woman that Thena didn't immediately recognize stopped her cart next to Thena and her mother.

Two boys, who looked old enough to be in school, held onto either side of the grocery cart. They glanced at Thena, boredom and indifference in their expressions.

"How are you doing, Sharla?" Margaret asked, helping Thena to remember who the woman was.

"Sharla Tate. It's good to see you again." Thena remembered her old schoolmate as being so thin and pretty. The woman before her was hardly either.

With a bandana wrapped around her hair, and a full-length dress that hung loosely over her ample figure, Sharla hardly looked like the same woman. Frown wrinkles formed around her mouth, and her dark eyes showed a raw bitterness that clogged any other emotions.

"Hmm." Sharla gave Thena the once-over, that gesture reminding her of the girl she'd gone to school with. "So you moving back here?"

"She's come home to help her mother," Margaret said before Thena could answer.

Thena didn't bother to look at her mother's face, knowing it beamed with confident pride. She'd made no commitment to stay here, and knew her mother wanted her to. But that was something they could discuss later.

"Well, you haven't come back to much." Sharla raised a shoulder, and dropped it lazily. "See you around."

She shuffled off, her children following without a word. Thena sensed pain and unhappiness float after the woman. She watched her for a moment before moving the cart forward in line toward the checkout.

"She sure has changed," she whispered so only her mother could hear.

"Lots of folks have." Her mother glanced at the magazines lined up on display next to the conveyer belt. She didn't elaborate.

"Your produce is looking shoddy." Perdy Williams was one of the few people Thena did remember.

The tall white woman didn't look any different from the last time Thena had seen her. One of the many locals, the thin woman with little figure to speak of handed money to the man at the register.

"Then don't buy them." The man working the register glared at Perdy.

Thena stared at him, trying to place how she knew him. Cold hatred surrounded the man. The emotions were so strong she had the urge to take a step or two back from him.

"Samuel Baker! I swear! I don't know what's gotten into you." Perdy Williams placed the paper sacks, full of her groceries, into her own cart, ignoring the boy at the end of the counter who tried to help her.

Thena didn't say anything while the man rang up their groceries. Her mother was unusually quiet too. Sam Baker glanced at her several times, as if trying to place her.

"He seemed positively evil," Thena whispered to her mom as they pushed the groceries out in the cart to her mother's car.

"Yes. Not that he ever had a lot of good in him, but he's changed." Her mother squinted against the morning sun. "And he isn't the only one. Evil has settled in Barren. That's what I was telling you about."

Thena glanced around the parking lot, and then up and down the quaint street that hadn't changed much over the years. "What do you mean?"

"You feel it. You see it." Her mother handed her sacks of groceries and Thena put them in the backseat. "I know you see it. Your powers have grown considerably. I knew they would. I need your help before it takes over."

"It? What's it?" Thena frowned at her mother, but then straightened when a young pregnant woman approached them with a couple of small children in tow.

The woman pulled her children close to her, away from Thena and her mother.

"Witch," one of the kids hissed, as they hurried by them.

Their actions shouldn't have fazed Thena. It was behavior she'd put up with since she was the age of those kids. If they hadn't teased and harassed her for the color of her skin, they'd ridiculed her for being born a witch. People could be terribly cruel, even children.

She wanted to say something. Let the mother know there was nothing to fear. Reassure the children that they would be safe around them. There were enough bad people in the world. She wasn't one of them. The pain never failed to needle at her every time she was snubbed. She hated it—absolutely hated it.

But she wouldn't let her feelings show. And she wouldn't bow her head in shame. Holding herself tall, and keeping her expression calm, she turned to help her mother into the car.

And that's when she saw him.

Standing across the parking lot, leaning against a small black car, Priapus watched her.

Thena froze.

"What is it?" her mother asked, looking up from the passenger seat, her cold hands gripping Thena's.

"Nothing, Mom. It's nothing." There was no way to explain him. Anything she could tell her mother would only make her worry or pry into her affairs. Either would be bad.

Priapus' look was intent. The parking lot wasn't that large, and although he'd parked toward the other side, she noticed his dark brooding stare. He wasn't too happy about something.

"We best get these groceries home. It's mighty warm in this car." Her mother let go of Thena and adjusted herself in her seat.

Thena closed her door and hurried around the car, stealing her gaze from Priapus. It was a free country. He could be wherever he wanted to be.

His gaze had unsettled her though. No—more than that. He'd branded her with hard, penetrating eyes that she swore saw through to her very soul.

She'd done nicely focusing on helping her mother all morning. It hadn't taken much more than a glance for Priapus to consume her thoughts. And that was so wrong. Nothing took over her mind unless she allowed it. No one controlled her life. And she'd always been happy with it that way.

"Stop in here." Her mother pointed to the gravel lot with one of the more rundown gas stations on it. "I don't like the tank getting below a quarter. It's not good for your engine, you know. And if Leroy is working, he'll give me a break in the price. Damned expensive gas."

"You get a break on gas?" Thena glanced at her mom. "No one gets a break on gas. He must be paying for it for you. Mom…do you have a boyfriend?"

Her mother snorted, pursing her lips. "Not everyone hates witches."

"True." She'd had quite a few friends back home in Kansas City who'd admired her calling. "But no one ever gave me a break in gasoline."

"You didn't have evil lurking everywhere." Her mother's gaze hazed over, her tone turning to a hushed whisper. "I can't protect everyone."

In spite of the fact that she knew her mother enjoyed the dramatics, a cold chill swept over Thena. She shook her head, refusing to let her mother make a drama out of ill-behaved people, and pulled into the gas station.

Her mother disappeared inside the station, leaving Thena to pump the gas.

"Thena Cooke! Well, I'll be damned. Thena Cooke, is that you?"

A thin woman walked around the gas station, her hair wrapped in a scarf at the back of her neck, and faded jeans hugging her thin legs.

Thena shaded her face with her hand, squinting in the sun, as the woman approached.

"If you don't remember me, I swear I'll smack you silly." The woman smiled, showing off large white teeth, and gaunt cheeks.

"Audry Simpson." Her memory clicked in, and at the same time she wondered what happened to the pretty young woman that she'd gone to high school with. "How are you doing?"

Audry's smile faded, dark shadows under her eyes indicating she'd had better days. "I'm doing okay. But I'm so glad you are here. Your mama said you were coming home. She said what she couldn't do that surely you could do."

Thena finished pumping the gas and secured the cap on the car. "Well, I—"

Thena didn't have a chance to question the woman before Audry took her by the wrist and started walking across the dusty gravel lot.

"You'll help me. Won't you help me, Thena?" Audry wasn't making any sense. "Your mama can't help me. But I just know that you can. Margaret said you were stronger."

"What are you talking about?" Thena managed to free her wrist and rubbed it while staring into the anxious expression on her high-school friend's face.

"It's my boy. He's five. You never have met him but he's the most precious child—best thing that ever happened to me." Worry lines spread around Audry's eyes.

An uncomfortable knot formed in Thena's tummy. She knew she was about to hear bad news. Instinctively, she put her hand on Audry's arm. Her old friend was loaded down with fear, something damn near panic. It rushed through Thena like a wildfire.

She pulled her hand away, rubbing her fingers together. "What's wrong?" she whispered.

Audry's blue eyes widened, hope filling her so quickly that the panic subsided. Thena wrinkled her brow. Audry was too easy to read.

"I knew you could help. Already you know something terrible is wrong. Did your mama tell you? Did she tell you about my little Nate?"

Thena shook her head. Her mother hadn't even mentioned Audry.

Audry put her hand to her mouth, simply studying Thena for a moment. Finally she looked down, licking her dry lips.

"Come with me. You'll see." She turned, returning toward the side of the building where Thena first saw her approach. "He used to chatter up a storm. Nate's teacher told me he was real smart, already reading."

Audry slowed when she got to the side of the gas station. Ahead of her, a small boy sat on the ground, his back to them. Icy chills rushed down Thena's spine.

"He won't come in the store while I'm working. He sits out here like that, not talking to anyone." Audry stared at her son for a moment and looked over her shoulder at Thena, the worry on her face drawing deep lines in her forehead. "You got the gift, Thena. You can fix him."

Thena didn't even know what was wrong with him. The child didn't move, didn't turn around when they'd walked up behind him. He simply sat there, cross-legged on the ground, staring at the empty field that spread out behind the gas station. An eerie chill crept through her, the behavior of the boy more than a little spooky.

Taking a step closer, she reached down and put her hand on the small boy's shoulder. "Nate?" she whispered.

The little boy turned around quickly, jumping to his feet. A piece of clothesline, knotted many times over, was wrapped around his small waist. Thena recognized the knots as part of a protection spell and guessed he wore it as something her mother might have suggested. It held no power though, and the way he wore it, it didn't even serve as a belt.

Thena wasn't sure she'd seen such outrage on a grown person's face before, let alone on a little boy's. He pointed a dirty finger at her, and for a moment, Thena thought his eyes glowed red.

"Get the fuck out of here." The voice that came out of the child didn't sound like a little boy's voice. It was raspy, deep, venomous.

Thena's heart thudded in her chest so hard she thought it would explode. Nate's actions completely took her off-guard.

"Nate. My baby." Audry started crying behind her. "That's the first time he's spoken in over a month. What's wrong with my baby?" she wailed.

Thena didn't look away from Nate. His eyes were wide, dilated, and glowing with an evil so raw that it absorbed his little body. There was no way a child his age could have so much anger in him, so much fury and hatred. He looked well-fed, cared-for. His clothes were simple but clean. And other than the fact that he'd been sitting in the dusty gravel, Thena could see that Audry took good care of him. There were no bruises, nothing to show he'd been abused.

Whatever consumed the child, it had taken over his entire existence.

Evil lurking everywhere. Her mother had said that right before going into the gas station. And she'd told her before she came down here that she needed Thena's help, that things weren't right.

Thena glared at whatever it was that was inside the young boy. "You are the one who is going to get the fuck out of here," she hissed, bending over so that she stared the boy in the face, and speaking quietly for only him to hear.

The boy stared at her for only a moment before collapsing to the ground, going limp at Thena's feet.

"Nate!" Audry screamed so loud that Thena jumped.

Her childhood friend hurried to the child, scooping him into her arms. At the same time something terribly cold rushed past Thena. And then it was gone. For some reason, she knew that the evil that had been inside the boy was no longer there. She walked up to her friend and stroked the hair from the boy's face.

"He's okay now," she whispered, watching long, soft lashes flutter over Nate's deep blue eyes.

He looked at her, and then up at his mother. "It's gone, Mommy. It's gone now."

Audry burst into tears, clinging to the child while she covered his face with kisses.

Thena turned, hearing footsteps behind her crunch over the gravel. Her mother appeared, an old man beside her who looked like he was at least ninety. If that was Leroy, he'd sure aged since she'd seen him last.

"Did you see?" Audry looked past her at the others. "Did you see how she fixed my baby? Oh Thena. You got the gift. Thank you. Thank you so much!"

Margaret Cooke took one look at her daughter, and then at the others. She reached out and stroked little Nate's forehead. "Didn't I tell you my daughter would be able to take care of it?"

"I really didn't do anything." Thena tried to make light of it.

She had done something though. Whatever passed by her, the icy cold sensation she'd experienced had come out of that child. Shivers rushed through her, and she stared at the ground suddenly feeling very tired.

"Take your boy on home," the older man said, giving Thena a strange look but then focusing on Audry. "I can manage around here for a few hours."

Audry smiled, her narrow cheeks damp from tears. "Thanks, Leroy. And Thena, you've saved my little boy's life. I won't forget that."

Thena didn't know what to say. She glanced at her mother who placed a reassuring hand on Thena's arm.

"Blessed be. You just cast out the devil, girl." Her mother looked proud enough to burst.

Thena just stared at her wide-eyed. Her good sense returned to her in a rush. That was the last thing she needed townsfolk to start saying.

"Bite your tongue, Mama. I did no such thing." Although she wasn't quite sure what had just happened.

"I saw little Nate. He was possessed hard and good and that's for sure. I knew you would be powerful. But my baby." Margaret reached up and stroked Thena's cheek, her eyes suddenly looking moist. "You left home before you were full-grown. I guessed you would be strong, so much stronger than me. But I never guessed—"

Her mother's words broke off, and she faked a cough so that Thena couldn't see that she'd teared up.

"Oh, Mom. You're making a big deal out of nothing." Thena couldn't help but feel a bit shaken though.

"Now that I know, there is much work to do." Margaret turned away, leaving Leroy with a pat on the arm and heading for her car before Thena could question her. "This whole town needs cleaning up."

Thena followed her, wondering if she actually did have what it took to cast evil out of a person. The foulness that had been in the boy still seemed to linger in the air. But something stronger slowly moved in on it. She looked up, the power immediately grabbing her attention, and across the street, Priapus stood watching her. The shiver that had rushed through her a minute before was replaced by a flushed heat. Her mouth went dry and she couldn't look away.

Chapter Seven

Priapus watched the demon fly through the air, cast out, exposed and vulnerable. He raised his hand, pointing his finger like a gun and aiming it at the demon.

"Pow," he said out loud, pulling the imaginary trigger in his hand.

The demon exploded, disappearing.

He returned his attention to Thena, who watched him over her car, looking more than just a bit curious. Raising an eyebrow, he blew on the edge of his finger, all the while watching her.

Her eyes widened at his small gesture. Whether or not she realized that he'd just killed the demon with his theatrics, he wasn't sure. At the moment he didn't care. She looked up toward the demon that fell to the ground like powdered dust, and then returned her attention to him.

Just watching her strut around her car, looking too high and mighty to give him the time of day, his cock stretched against his leg, throbbing with need to know her better.

He'd never known a human to have that much power. No one could see him, and he hadn't willed Thena to be able to see him, yet she did. And she noticed the demon explode in the air. Humans had never bothered to develop their abilities to see beings around them, other than themselves.

Something didn't sit right here, and Priapus had a feeling that if he didn't get to the bottom of it soon, things could get ugly. Thena had just drawn attention to herself by ridding the demon from the boy. No matter that she'd done a good thing. The demons would catch wind of what she'd done, and they would retaliate.

His insides hardened at the thought of those fucking demons getting their hands on Thena. It was time to intervene. She had no idea what she was getting herself into and he wouldn't see her get hurt.

But he would have to be careful, making a scene would only make the talk spread faster. Already he sensed the demons were outraged, arguing among themselves as to how to handle this matter.

For a moment his decision brought him pause. It mattered to him that Thena be taken care of. He barely knew the woman, yet something inside him stirred whenever he laid eyes on her. She was strong, beautiful, and filled with a passion for life.

Times had hit her hard, and she'd come home to her mama on the pretense of helping her. But he knew that like him, she'd been humiliated and had run. He related to those hard feelings and wanted to reach out to her, share his experiences, talk more with her, learn what made her tick.

Another time, another place flashed through his mind, a memory almost forgotten. Priapus watched thoughtfully as Thena climbed into her car, ignoring him. Somehow the time when he'd helped a small boy popped into his head. It had been so long ago, over a thousand Earth years, and in a land so far away and no longer recognized in today's world.

He'd been so much younger, so full of himself, so cocky with his god-standing among the people. At the moment the name of the maiden who'd captured his attention eluded him. The gathering place in the village had been the town pub, located in the heart of the main street. He'd been outside, boasting of his protective skills, enjoying his praises being sung by the men surrounding him.

"We are strong because of you, Priapus. All we have is because of you." They worshipped him at that time, and he'd reveled in every moment of it.

An image of the young maiden appeared in his mind, running down the main street, holding her dress up so she wouldn't trip, showing off her thin ankles.

"Help me!" she'd screamed. "Please! I need help. He'll die for sure!"

The men around him turned on her quickly, the daughter of a shunned family.

"Who are you, wench?" they'd tormented her. "Why would we lift a finger to help a family who refuses to worship our gods?"

She'd stopped in front of him, falling to her knees, her bountiful breasts heaving while she'd gasped for breath. Her face was tearstained and her hair disheveled.

"Master. I beg you." She'd thrown herself at his feet, her small hands daring to touch his shoes. "I can't help him. But you can. Please."

Priapus had lifted her, carrying her through the air, calming her with soothing words while they flew in front of the townsfolk back to her secluded home where her younger brother had fallen into a deep well. It hadn't taken any effort to lift the child, free him from his entrapment, mend his broken bones. The family had been so grateful.

And the town had turned their back on him.

Priapus straightened, shoving the memory from his head. Someone hurried out of the gas station, approaching Thena and her mother before they could drive off. Another car pulled into the station, a young man getting out for gas and quickly becoming part of the conversation between the person standing outside the cars, and Thena and her mother.

"Thena, don't leave yet. Leroy just told me what you did." The older woman who hurried around the front of the car looked vaguely familiar. Thena watched her approach, letting the car idle.

The woman's ample breasts bounced while she almost ran toward Thena, waving her hand, with a way too cheerful smile on her face.

Her mother groaned next to her. At the same time, Tommy Joe Baker pulled his pickup truck to a stop and hopped out, shading his eyes with his hand as he stared into her mother's car.

"Thena Cooke? Is that you?" Tommy Joe asked in his thick drawl that sounded the same as he had in school when she was a girl.

"Of course it's her," the woman who now stood at Thena's door snapped. "And you can't just be leaving now, Thena Cooke. Not with what you've done."

"Maxine Poller, here you go expecting the world set straight in a minute," Margaret muttered, yet loud enough for Maxine to hear her.

"It's good to see you again, Maxine. How is your family?" Thena remembered her now.

Maxine Poller had children who had been a few years younger than Thena. Their families hadn't mixed much, but she'd seen her in town when she and her mother went shopping back when Thena was growing up.

She smiled up at the woman, who had a shrewd eye on her.

Maxine bent over, almost sticking her head in the car. She peered over at Tommy Joe, as if wanting to say something she feared would be overheard.

"There are more. I'm sure your mama has told you that." Maxine spoke in a hushed whisper, her dark hand gripping Thena's, which was on the steering wheel.

Thena stared at Maxine's hand for a moment. The woman's skin was warm, moist, her hand a lot larger than Thena's. The woman was scared, her fear running through her like sweat.

"There are more what?" She looked at Maxine, seeing worry etched in her brow.

It was just as it had been with her mother. Implications of something going on, but no clear cut-and-dry explanations. She was getting tired of this and wished she could just sort through the woman's thoughts, understand fully what would have her running to their car, grabbing Thena and implying such urgency.

She glanced past Maxine for a brief moment, Priapus catching her attention while he stood across the street, his arms crossed, looking rather displeased while he watched her.

Like he had anything to be upset about. He wasn't being bombarded with old biddies who hadn't given her the time of day until she'd done something odd.

At the same moment Maxine looked past Thena at her mother, and then outside the car, watching while Tommy Joe headed into the station to pay for his gas.

"There are more people who got something wrong in them—just like little Nate." Maxine met her gaze.

"And you can't go around fixing people who don't want fixed," Margaret cut in, her tone harsh. "Maxine, we aren't miracle workers and you let go of my daughter."

Thena watched Maxine. The woman didn't want to let go of her. There was an urgent determination running through the older woman that was strong enough to smell. Maxine wanted to yank her out of the car and put the town back to how it used to be. Her feelings were strong enough to cut with a knife.

Thena caught her breath in her throat, her heart suddenly missing a beat. Had she just managed to read the woman's mind, or had she just guessed that was what Maxine was thinking?

"I'll tell you everything I know." When Maxine looked past her again at her mother, Thena sensed hostility. "But you come on over to my place. I won't have your mama pestering at me to stay out of things. You know damned good and well, Margaret Cooke, that things ain't right. Just cuz you can't fix them. Don't you dare stop your daughter if she can do it."

"How dare you take a tone like that with me," Margaret hissed, her defenses up immediately. "You know well and good I want this town fixed, too. Thena just got home. She needs time."

"Enough. Both of you." Thena gave her mother a pleading look, and then turned to Maxine, opening the car door while the woman took a step backward. She stood outside the car, smiling at the older lady. "I want to help. And I will if I can. But right now I don't understand any of this."

She wanted Maxine to calm down, knowing from past experience that if someone got her mother's dander up, life would be hell while her mom paced the house, threatening all kinds of evil spells that she would never perform on anyone.

Maxine relaxed noticeably, a pleasant smile appearing on her face. "I'm already feeling better talking to you. And you come over now. I'm serious. I'm going to arrange for you to see my son. He ain't right. And no one is going to tell me he don't want to be fixed. He was a good boy. There is something going on in this town. You just hang out a few days. You'll see. I can't explain it. But you'll see."

Thena glanced past Maxine, distracted suddenly when she realized that Priapus was no longer across the street. Maxine followed her gaze when Thena noticed him driving into the gas station and pulling up to the pump behind her. He got out of the car, wearing simple blue jeans and a T-shirt that stretched over hard chest muscles.

He looked different than he had before. Now his hair fell straight, not quite to his shoulders, layered slightly, giving him a casual appearance. From the long hair that he'd had when she first met him in Kansas City, to the business look that he'd sported in the airport and in her mother's yard, and now a look that made him appear a local, she wondered at the limits of his magic. When he glanced her way, those soft green eyes, the one thing that remained the same about him, captured her with enough heat to make her heart pick up a beat.

I'm watching you. She swore she heard him whisper the words into her ears. *Be careful where you tread.*

Maxine had already looked away, reaching out and giving Thena's wrist a squeeze. "You call me. And whatever you do, don't say anything to Tommy Joe. He's one of them."

With that, she hurried back around the car, keeping her head down when Tommy Joe gave her a harsh look and then turned his attention to Thena.

"Get in the car, Thena." Her mother had a warning tone that grabbed her attention.

"Don't you run off without saying hi to me, Thena Cooke." Tommy Joe sauntered around their car.

He was even taller than he'd been in high school, his body still long and lanky. She attempted a smile, putting her hand on the car door handle to let her mother know she wasn't ignoring her. She couldn't just run and be rude to one of her true dear friends from childhood.

"It's good to see you, Tommy Joe." Thena smiled up at the man but then when her mother cleared her throat inside the car, she added for her benefit, "I was just getting ready to head home with Mama and a bunch of groceries."

Something unpleasant seeped through her when she stared into Tommy Joe's icy blue eyes. He didn't return her smile and moved until he stood close enough to her that she couldn't open her car door without physically pushing him out of the way. He unnerved her, standing so close. At the same time, she sensed Priapus behind her. His power rushed around her, seeming to protect her from the closeness of Tommy Joe.

"So you're staying with your mama, then?" Anger seemed to radiate from him. Even his posture was tight, rigid. "Maybe I'll stop by there in a bit."

"The milk is getting warm." Margaret spoke loud enough for Tommy Joe to hear her clearly. "You get in this car now, girl."

He took a step backwards. "You take your mother on home now. Drive carefully. We wouldn't want anything to happen to a pretty lady and her mother."

Thena frowned when he stepped back to let her get in the car. She didn't say anything, but got in and watched him return to his truck.

"Something's wrong with him." She hadn't meant to speak out loud.

Tommy Joe turned to look at her again before climbing into his truck. His expression was almost fierce, as if he'd overheard her, although she doubted very much that he had. The boy she remembered from grade school and high school had been a friendly, carefree sort. Tommy Joe had a deep crush on her for a while until his daddy had put a stop to it, announcing none too quietly that no boy of his would date a black woman.

She remembered how awkward he had been as a boy, not attractive, and with hardly any friends. But he'd been such a good friend, willing to hang out with her when the other kids teased her.

The man walking away from her now looked hardened, almost fierce, like he was highly pissed off and aching for a good fight.

"There's something wrong with a lot of people around here." Her mother sounded defeated, tired.

Thena turned her attention to her, reaching for her hand. "Is that why you called me home? Why Gramma wanted me back here so badly?"

"It's too much for the two of us to handle. I don't know magic to fix this." Her mother shook her head, watching while Tommy Joe drove off. He glanced back at them again, his frown deepening. Her mother squeezed her hand, and then let go. "I didn't know if you'd be able to help or not. Now I do. But there are a lot of them. Decisions need to be made."

Thena glanced at her side mirror, knowing Priapus was still behind her. His power almost soothed her, reassuring her somehow that he would protect her if she simply asked.

But did she need protection from him as well?

Her heart skipped a beat, remembering how it felt to be in his arms. The thought gave her goose bumps, while excitement over possibly seeing him again put a lump in her tummy.

Priapus got in his car when Thena drove off.

There was no way he would allow them to gang up on her. No matter that she had powers stronger than any human should have. He doubted she knew how conniving demons could be.

He would take her under his protection. The only problem was Thena was proving to be mighty damned stubborn.

Thena and her mom drove in silence for a while as she headed down the narrow county road toward her mom's house.

"Why did you think I would be so much stronger than you?" she asked, breaking the silence.

Margaret took a long look at her daughter. Thena glanced over at her, her silver hair sprinkled with black and piled high on her head. Concern and worry clouded her mother's soft brown eyes.

"Why should I be any different than you?" Thena pushed, a feeling coming over her that her mom had something to say and wasn't sure how to say it.

"It's just a feeling that I have," her mother said quietly, obviously holding something back.

Thena pursed her lips. Her mom might be stubborn, but so was she.

Pulling into the drive in front of her mother's home, Thena sighed heavily. "So you tried to make little Nate better?"

Margaret scowled at Thena. "You know I did. I tried every spell and concoction that I could think of. Your Gramma did too. You saw the rope around his waist. We tied so many knots trying to get that evil out of him. Nothing worked."

She got out of the car, shutting the door firmly behind her, and headed to the house.

Well, hell. She'd offended her mother by succeeding in doing something her mother couldn't. Thena reached behind her, grabbing the sacks of groceries and then hurried after her mother.

"Mom." She shut the front door quickly behind her with her foot, finding her mother already in the kitchen, placing candles on the table. "I'm sure I can't do more than you can. I had no idea what was wrong with Nate. I just acted. There wasn't time to think."

She thought about the evil voice that had come from the child and shuddered. Whatever had left him, Priapus had destroyed. The icy chill that rushed past her had dissipated when he'd pointed his finger at it. She hadn't been able to destroy it, and she had no idea what it was. But he'd destroyed it with a mere gesture of his finger. She didn't have near his strength.

Not to mention how his appearance kept changing. Thena could style her hair, change the type of clothes she wore, apply different makeup. But that wasn't magic. There was no way she could do what Priapus could do.

Thinking about him though, made her want to feel his strength. He was such a mystery, claiming to be a god. And not just any god. Priapus was known for having a cock twice the length of any other man. He was the god of fertility, the protector. She ran her tongue over her lips, her mouth suddenly too moist. Would he really have a cock that size?

Dear God. She'd only had sex with a handful of men her entire life. There was no way she would be able to handle a man that well-endowed.

What was she thinking?

She gave herself a mental shake, focusing on her mother who was now in the process of lighting almost a dozen candles she'd gathered and put on the kitchen table.

Hurrying to put the groceries on the counter before she dropped them, she willed the excited heat that suddenly rushed through her to subside.

"Thena," her mother said, not looking up. She moved around the table with her long wooden match, continuing to light the candles. "We create spells, practice the wording, use our tools—the candles, our herbs, the concoctions we make, because it helps us. Reciting our incantations, calling forth the gods, helps us clear our minds, focus on the task we're trying to remedy."

Thena nodded, putting the milk in the refrigerator. "Yes. I'm not five. I know that."

"Don't you sass me, girl. This is important." Margaret puffed her small chest out, her petite frame draped with the long loose-fitting dress she wore. She puckered her lips together, pointing at Thena with the lighted, long wooden match. "I wanted to talk to you alone, before Gramma gets back. You don't need those props. Don't you see?"

"What would you want to talk to me about that Gramma can't hear?" Thena shook her head. "I've always practiced the craft properly. I don't even think of my tools as props. They are…well, they're part of me."

"Your Gramma knows I'm having this conversation with you." Margaret sighed. "I just wanted to have it without her putting in her two cents."

Carefully blowing out the match, Margaret placed it in the sink and took a small cigar box out of her cabinet. Thena knew it well as the cherished box where her mother kept her blessed herbs. Her mother set the box on the table, running her fingers gingerly over the top of it before opening it. The simple act brought back many memories of her mother performing spells throughout Thena's life—always the small cigar box was close at hand.

"What is it that you want to talk to me about?" Thena wasn't surprised her mother wanted to talk before Gramma showed up.

Her Gramma always had strong opinions about everything, a trait she'd passed down to her daughter, and Thena as well. She chewed her lip, something telling her that her mother was anxious about something.

Her mother opened the box, allowing the fresh scent of her special mixture of ground herbs to fill the kitchen. She pinched at the herbs, her bony fingers picking up clumps of the herbs and slowly creating a circle around the candles.

"We need to talk about who you are."

"What do you mean, Mom?" A nervous twang stabbed at her gut. "I know who I am. I'm your daughter. And I'm a witch, right?"

Margaret nodded, not looking at her but focusing on her task. "I raised you that way. But it's not *who* you are."

"What's that supposed to mean?" Thena frowned, her attention shooting from her mother's determined expression to her mother's fingers, deftly creating a circle around the candles with her herbs.

Margaret shook her head firmly, closing her eyes once she'd completed the circle. Reaching for Thena's hand, she gripped it firmly, the familiar touch of her mom's smooth, cool skin comforting under most circumstances, a hand that had caressed her and removed all fears for so many years. At the moment though, Thena was frustrated. Her mother was sidestepping questions. And Thena hated it when she did that.

Margaret held her free hand over the flames of the candles. "Earth. Wind. Fire. Air. All of the elements are within us. Our spirits soar, welcoming your strength. We can do anything and go anywhere. Earth. Wind. Fire. Air. Your powers within us, we can go anywhere."

Her mother began swaying, for a moment humming quietly. Thena held her free hand out too, feeling the flames dance under her palm, warm her skin, and slowly move through her.

The strength of both of them filled the air around her. She inhaled slowly, welcoming the power, sensing her mother's strength. Older and wiser, her mother's concern and worry began filtering through her. She embraced it, focusing on the steady beat of her own heart, doing her best to soothe her mother's fears for her with her mind.

"Keeper of that holy gate. Protector between this world and the next." Her mother's voice was low, husky, chanting the words in a melodic tone. "The world of gods we call upon. Open please, and come to us."

Thena didn't remember having ever heard her mother chant these words before. Her mother was asking for a cross gate.

"Meet us again. Your aid we need. Your aid we request. Protector between this world and the next." The warmth in her mother's hand grew, seeping up Thena's arm.

She felt her mother's pulse, their heartbeats sounding as one.

"Having come before. Now we beg for you again. Your strength and advice, your wisdom and security. As you have before, give to us again," her mother almost whispered in a singsong voice.

The flames danced under her hand. Their heat almost burned her and Thena concentrated on her breathing, slowing it, soothing the dance of the flames. The heat subsided.

But the strength in the room grew. She no longer felt her mother's hand. Something in the room had changed, the air full of a new presence, a strange sensation that seemed familiar, oddly reminiscent of a time Thena couldn't remember.

"Our worlds combine. Our worlds are one. Our worlds combine." Her mother's voice seemed far away, chanting the same thing over and over again in a soft whisper.

Thena could hardly breathe from the strength that seemed to press against her, push into her until she almost felt claustrophobic in her mother's kitchen.

Opening her eyes, she realized she'd drifted off of the floor, and was too close to the ceiling. Her mother still had her eyes closed, both of her hands now over the candles, repeating her mantra with her expression wrinkled in determination.

Thena lowered herself to the ground, silently grateful her mother hadn't seen her float. It wasn't something she did consciously, and didn't want her mother's concentration shattered by her daughter's unusual behavior.

"Who are you calling?" she whispered, watching her mother sway back and forth.

Her mother smiled, her eyes still closed. "He is here. Do you feel him?"

She definitely felt something.

"Who?" she asked again.

Her mother opened her eyes, smiling. Her face glowed with a flush that made her look so much younger. She looked excited, full of life, a look she hadn't seen on her mother's face in a long time.

Patting her thin hands over her silver hair, she smoothed it, and then straightened her dress. Then Margaret glanced around the room, resting her gaze on the back door.

"He is here," she repeated, whispering, sounding very odd.

Margaret moved to the back door, looking through the window in the door at the yard out back. Thena could feel her anxiousness, an excitement that mixed with the strange power that had filled the room. If she didn't know better, she would guess that her mother was showing the excitement of a schoolgirl, waiting for her beau to show up.

Along with her mother's suddenly weird behavior, the power that wrapped around her stole the air from the room. This wasn't the same strength she'd felt with Priapus. His energy had been raw, carnal, dominating and determined. What she experienced now seemed more steady, like a hard summer rain, continuous and firm.

The candles' flames danced furiously, swaying as if caught by a strong breeze. Margaret opened the back door, staring outside while she pressed her hand to her cheek.

"Mom. Tell me what's going on." Thena hadn't experienced anything like this other than when Priapus had come to her.

Her mother turned around, reaching for Thena. "Come with me. It's time that you met your father."

Thena just stared at her mother, sure that she hadn't heard her correctly. "My father?" she whispered.

She'd never had a father. Never. As long as she could remember, it had just been her and her mom. Whenever she'd asked in the past, her mother had told her it had just been a fling. A short and hot romance that should never have been, but had blessed her with Thena. Her mother had never given her a name, a description—nothing.

"What are you talking about?" she gasped, too stunned to even put meaning to her mother's words.

But her mother didn't answer her. Instead she turned and walked out the back door.

Chapter Eight

Priapus looked up when someone suddenly appeared at the entrance to the fence surrounding Margaret's home. Thena's mom didn't live out in the country, but she was definitely on the edge of town, the narrow county road quiet for the most part, with the houses spaced far from each other. If he'd walked up to the house, Priapus would have noticed him before that moment.

Floating to the ground, Priapus straightened, the man meeting his gaze. His expression changed when he recognized Priapus, concern creasing his brow.

Thena's mom's chanting hadn't made a lot of sense but he'd listened intently. Her powers were weak, nothing more than an average witch who believed completely in her own strength.

Her belief was stronger than her powers, but they'd grabbed the attention of someone.

The older man stopped when he reached the gate, his gaze narrowing on Priapus. After only a moment, Priapus recognized the god standing before him.

"What are you doing here?" the man asked, not speaking out loud, but sending his thoughts.

"Triton. It's good to see you again." Priapus nodded, sharing his thoughts, well, some of them, while searching the man's face, looking for some indication that Thena might be his daughter.

And if she was… Well, damn it to all of the hells. That would make Thena the daughter of a god, a mortal who'd been conceived by one of the immortals. He shook his head, wanting to kick himself for not thinking it a possibility. It sure did explain why her powers were so strong. Thena was only half witch, her other half, unexplored, was much stronger.

Triton lowered his head slightly, a silent acknowledgment of the greeting. "Under most circumstances, I'd say the same of you, Priapus. But why are you here, keeping watch over this house?"

A protector's instinct rushed through Priapus. He gazed at Triton, unwilling to share any reason why he might be here. It was none of the man's damn business.

Triton gave him a quick once-over, searching for answers that Priapus had no intention of giving him. They stared at each other for a moment, Priapus sensing a paternal instinct rising up that didn't faze him.

Triton was a good man, an immortal that Priapus had never had a beef with. Throughout all of time, their paths hadn't crossed that often. He wouldn't counter him now either. Whether he'd fathered Thena or not, it was obvious by the confusion he sensed from Thena over her mom's words, that he'd never taken the time to know his daughter.

"Because I choose to," he told him simply, and then turned when Margaret walked around the side of the house.

"Triton," she called out, the joy on her face making her glow.

Priapus adjusted himself so that she couldn't see him, but held his ground, ignoring the hard glare that Triton gave him before turning his attention to the older woman.

"Margaret," Triton said quietly. He walked toward her, holding his arms out.

She walked into them, embracing him with the tenderness of an old lover.

Thena walked around the house, hesitant, watching her mother hug a man she'd never laid eyes upon before. Her heart slammed in her chest at the sight of Priapus. He watched the small scene, his expression masked, although something told her he wasn't pleased. That bit of knowledge had her curious. But there was no way she could explore it at the moment. When her mother let go of the man, turning to her with a bright smile on her face, she realized that she didn't see Priapus. Thena wondered if the man with her knew he was there.

"Thena," her mom said, holding her hand out to her. "This is Triton. And before you say anything, we need him here. The time has come for you to fully understand your powers. What happened today won't go unnoticed. And there was a reason you were able to do what your Gramma and I can't do."

Thena stared at the man who had his arm around her mother. He was tall, thick-shouldered, appearing to be around the same age as her mother. He was white, with silver hair cut in a crew cut, reminding her of an old sailor, with a well-weathered expression on his face. He wasn't bad-looking, his appearance clean and friendly enough.

But too many unanswered questions swirled around in her mind at the moment. She had a father. Her mother knew him, and with nothing more than a simple incantation had been able to call him to them without ceremony. Yet over the years, there'd never been mention of him.

And then there was Priapus, standing there, watching her, waiting for her reaction along with her mother and this stranger who'd just been thrown in her face.

This was all simply too much.

"I don't believe this, Mom." Anger swirled up in her before she could stop it. "You don't just throw some stranger in my face and tell me that he's my dad. Where was he when I was growing up?"

Her voice rose as she spoke, emotions coming at her too strong to control. It took most of her strength to keep her feet on the ground. Powers surged through her, wanting to take over.

"Thena..." Triton began, extending his hand to her.

Thena took a step backwards. "A few simple words and he's right here." She glared at her mom. "Yet you never bothered to tell me a thing about him when I was a child. Don't you think I would have liked to have had a dad?"

She turned on them, ignoring her mother when she called out to her. Outrage swam through her. She slapped her hand against the side of one of the large trees that shaded the side of the house, and ignored the tree limb that fell to the ground behind her, crashing loudly. At the moment she didn't care that her outrage had sent the large branch to the ground.

All she wanted to do was release her anger, her fury that her mother had known all along where her father was. He came right to her when she called him. How often had he come around when she was growing up? Had he seen her as a child and not let her know he was her father?

Tears burned at her eyes and she started running, taking off into the field behind her mother's house. No matter that her feet left the ground after a few moments. She was too damned mad to care that it was broad daylight.

She had a father. Some man named Triton was her father. And a simple incantation had brought him straight to her.

Triton. Her mother had called him Triton.

There was a sea god named Triton.

Thena fell to the ground, hitting it hard, her skin burning instantly as she tumbled against the hard dirt.

She was the daughter of a god.

Priapus glared at Triton, letting him know with his thoughts in no uncertain terms that he better not chase after Thena. He then rushed after her, feeling her pain even before he caught up with her.

"Are you okay?" He landed next to her, reaching to lift her up before she could stop him.

Strong arms lifted her, Priapus pulling her against his strong chest.

Thena stiffened. "Leave me alone," she muttered, feeling incredibly sorry for herself and not wanting to share her self-pity at the moment.

Not to mention she knew she looked like shit with her tearstained cheeks and swollen eyes from crying.

"I have no intention of leaving you alone." Priapus knelt next to her, wrapping his arm around her so that she wouldn't pull away. "And you know that."

"I don't know anything, not anymore." It dawned on her that she'd flown to this spot, and looking through her tear-blurred vision, she couldn't see her mom's house.

They were out in the middle of the country, the town of Barren a couple of miles away. Her mind spun with the knowledge that she'd traveled so quickly in such a short time. Nothing like this had ever happened to her before. She hadn't given it any thought, just raced away from the unacceptable situation.

And Priapus had followed her easily. These were powers she'd never imagined. And even though she'd committed them, she was overwhelmed with the reality that she was way out of her league.

She looked up at him. He was so damned handsome, his green eyes soft, filled with concern, although she didn't miss the passion that made them appear like deep pools, so rich and so deep. He wanted her. There was no missing that. His expression remained calm, his strong facial features relaxed and controlled. It wasn't as easy to read him as it had been the people at the gas station earlier. She wondered if he knew her thoughts, if he could read her like an open book.

Immediately her mouth went dry, and she looked down, only to rest her gaze on his hard abdomen. Then her thoughts went to where they'd been earlier, wondering about the size of his cock. Her heart began thudding in her chest.

Priapus ran his hand down her arm, loving how soft her skin was. The simple sundress she wore twisted slightly on her body, giving him a wonderful view of her cleavage. Soft mounds rose and fell with her breathing. He ran his finger against her brow, willing her to look up at him again.

"Thena," he whispered, knowing he scared and excited her all at once.

More than anything he wanted that dress off of her. He wanted to see her body laid out before him. Memories of how she'd looked the first time he'd laid eyes on her made him hard as a rock. Thena's breath caught, her body stilling against his, and he knew she felt his hardness press against her.

"It's okay," she said, slowly moving out of his arms and standing. She still didn't look at him. "If you were able to come after me so quickly, then I'm sure Triton will too. I don't need to be taken care of. And regardless of what my mother thinks, I don't need a man I've never met before explaining to me why I was able to cast out the devil—or whatever that thing was in Nate."

So she'd figured out that Triton was also a god. He shouldn't have been surprised.

"You have no idea what you're battling." He held his hand out to her, not taking her into his arms again, but standing also, and allowing her to decide if she would place her hand in his or not. "There are demons everywhere around here. They aren't *the* devil. But they are fighting for that rank. And they'll take out Earth in the process in their efforts. You cast out one, but that just outraged the others. They will come after you. And you don't have the knowledge to fight them."

Thena did look up at him then, her soft brown eyes melting like warm chocolate. The sun captured the radiance in her black hair, making it shine. Her smooth caramel skin and soft features made her an image of beauty that captured his breath as he stared at her.

She brushed her dress off, taking her time in deciding how to respond. For the most part, none of what he just said made any sense. It was clear he had a better understanding of the elements than she did. But she accepted that there was good and evil out there. And if she had powers that she hadn't explored before, she would learn how to do that. Before any of that happened though, Priapus and her mother would understand that she wasn't defenseless and in need of protection.

"I've been fighting people all of my life." She put her hands on her hips, fighting not to let him distract her when he looked down at her. "I've been picked on for being black, and shunned for being a witch. Don't tell me that I don't have the knowledge to fight back. No one is going to take me down."

Priapus grabbed her arms, squeezing them at her side while he lifted her slightly. "We aren't talking about fighting prejudice here, or ignorance. We are fighting hatred at its extreme core, from the depths of where hatred stems."

Thena brought her arms up quickly, pushing him away and stepping back. She turned on him and began walking back toward town. He was on her immediately, grabbing her arm and forcing her to face him.

"I'm not afraid," she hissed, her breathing coming so hard she almost panted. "I saw what was in that little boy. And if there are others out there like him, and I can help, then I'll do it. But I don't need protection from you, or my mother—or some man claiming to be my father whom I've never even met before."

Priapus pulled her to him, wrapping his arm around her so she couldn't escape. "You can help. And I can help too. But first we are going to find out what truly lies in you. Because my Thena, you are much, much more than just a witch."

"I am not your Thena," she said, stressing every word.

Priapus claimed her mouth before she could utter more. He branded her with a heat that made her legs go limp. She gripped his shirt in her hands, unable to find the strength or the desire to push him away. He was reaching straight through her, clamping down on her heart, and she wasn't sure she wanted to stop him.

Without a thought she opened her mouth to him, allowed him to deepen the kiss, explore her with a touch that was tender and at the same time demanding.

His hands moved over her back, caressing, stroking, adding to the fire that already simmered deep inside her. She was drowning, falling so fast there was no way she would surface anytime soon. The way he devoured her mouth, he would rob her of all sane thought within a matter of moments.

His cock grew between them, thick, long and throbbing. She knew she wasn't thinking clearly when the thing seemed to stretch over the length of her body. He'd claimed to be Priapus though, and she knew the god was known for the size of his penis.

Butterflies took flight in her stomach, a twisting sense of apprehension and excitement building within her.

"Holy crap," she cried out the second his mouth left hers, leaving her gasping for breath.

He trailed a steamy path of kisses along her cheek to her ear and then nibbled at the sensitive lobe. Wells of passion bubbled, threatening to flow over and flood her insides. His lips caressed the side of her neck, finding her most sensitive areas. Electrical currents shot through her straight to her pussy. She fisted his shirt in her hands, doing everything she could just to hold on.

This shouldn't be happening. Her life had just been thrown one hell of a curveball, and the last thing she needed to do was add a new relationship to that. The magic he worked on her right now made it impossible to tell him to stop.

"It's not magic," he whispered into her ear, his breath sending chills rushing through her at the speed of lightning.

Thena growled, although the urge to giggle hit her at the same time. "If you can read my mind, then I can read yours," she challenged, letting her head fall back when he traced a hot, moist trail with his tongue down her neck.

The moist pressure of his mouth brushing over her pulse and the sensitive skin at her nape, made it almost impossible to focus her thoughts. She'd never attempted any type of telepathy. All she could think to do was listen, and wonder if she imagined hearing him in her mind, or if those were actually thoughts. And even then, it seemed he spoke reassuring words, praising her, begging to adore her. Words too easily made up by her lust-driven body.

Priapus released her, moving his arms so that his hands covered her breasts. His long fingers gripped them, giving them a slight tug and squeeze at the same time.

Her nipples hardened against his flesh, making his blood pressure rise to a critical point. Blood pumped through him so hard he had a hard time keeping his thoughts focused.

Thena had no idea what powers she possessed, and neither did he. One thing he did know, in the heat of passion, she might suddenly do something completely unexpected. He needed to make love to her more than he needed to breathe at the moment. But along with that, pushing her emotions, seducing her and bringing out the natural passion within her, would bring forth her powers, allow her to relax enough to set them free. And when they united, when he entered and released himself in her, it would combine their strength, giving her part of him and him part of her.

Her mother and newfound father wouldn't turn her into some experiment. He wouldn't allow her to be tested to find out how strong she was. That would only belittle her. And Thena was too intelligent, too strong, too damned beautiful to be insulted that way.

His way would be much better.

"I'm a test?" She was trying to read his mind, but with her senses wrapped in such a sensual fog, it was almost an impossible task to concentrate. "Who is insulting me?"

Thena managed to press against his chest, backing up a little, although she almost staggered backwards. Priapus moved to close the space between them.

"I won't have anyone determining the strength of your powers," he told her, knowing she needed to hear the truth from him. He ran his hands down her bare shoulders, grabbing the straps to her dress and dragging them down her arms. "You will learn your own strengths, and share them when you decide, not when others decide for you."

Priapus pulled the straps of her dress down her arms, tugging the material so that it glided over her breasts, revealing her to him. His gaze lowered instantly and he sucked in a breath. He looked very pleased, making her feel even sexier when his breath came heavier, and more staggered.

"Is this a decision I am making, or you are making for me?" she asked, her voice now a husky whisper.

She felt so alive at the moment, so incredibly in control. The way he drooled over the sight of her exposed breasts made her feel beautiful, wanted, cherished.

"The decision to use your powers is always yours." He looked distracted though, his gaze lowered, his hands now caressing her full round breasts.

Thena didn't want to have this conversation while he was teasing her into a frenzy. And it was quite clear she would have to fight him off to get him to stop. The way his large hands caressed her, his fingers rubbing her nipples, she knew there was no way she could sound convincing if she asked him to leave her alone.

Priapus loved how her face flushed such a lovely dark rose. The smoothness of her skin, her narrow neck and shoulders, and her full breasts that swelled in his hands was better than finding a buried treasure no one knew was even there. Thena was the catch of a lifetime, full of life yet with an almost innocent air about her. Men prayed to be given such a gift that he had standing in front of him.

"I know that I can make my own decisions," she said, finally able to make her mouth move to form words.

He groaned instead of commenting, lowering his head so that he could suckle in one of her nipples, teasing it with his tongue and then scraping the sensitive flesh with his teeth.

Thena squealed, gripping a hold of him with all the strength she had. Her nipples were more sensitive than any other part of her body, and he'd just sent a tidal wave of lust gushing through her to her cunt.

"And I know you can, too," he told her, whispering into the swell between her breasts. "So tell me now, do you want this?"

For a moment Thena was confused. Did she want what?

It wasn't fair to make her think while his tongue traced wicked paths over her feverish flesh. Priapus had worked her dress down to her waist, and now stretched his hands over her outer thighs, his fingers pressing into her skin.

"This isn't fair." The fiery heat burning through her seemed to intensify with every pulse of her heart. "You're manipulating me somehow."

Priapus chuckled, his fingers brushing over her thighs, working their way underneath her dress.

"The only powers in effect here are ones of mutual attraction. I promise." His green eyes swarmed with lust, captivating her, making it impossible to look away when he met her gaze. "Unless you have cast a spell on me, my dear."

Thena managed to shake her head, her body almost trembling when he moved his hands, gripping her ass.

"Then answer my question," he demanded, raising her dress so that it now bundled around her waist like a tangled belt.

Thena frowned, too distracted by the fresh air that now brushed against her exposed ass and pussy. The thin fabric of her panties, soaked and clinging to her, did nothing to make her feel less vulnerable. Priapus lowered his head again, his hair tickling her skin as he kissed her collarbone.

"What?" She fought to steady herself when she wanted to collapse into him.

Her hands spread across his chest, feeling the heat of his body, the strong muscles that bulged under his shirt.

"Do you want this?" he asked her again, his breath torturing her skin.

There was no way she could deny the passion that rippled through her like a fast-moving stream, tumbling and twisting so quickly that all she could do was hold on.

"Yes." Her voice sounded foreign, thick like honey yet raspy, almost a whisper.

She should ask what he was offering. Too many thoughts rushed at her at once though, and all of them in a foggy haze of lust. Her body cried for release, the growing pressure in her craving satisfaction.

The back of her legs hit something, and Thena looked over her shoulder, confused. A beautiful king-size bed, complete with brass head and floorboard, and too many stuffed pillows to count, had appeared behind her. It looked magnificent in the middle of the field, yet so oddly out of place.

"Lay down," Priapus instructed, holding on to her while she sat down on the bed, her face a whirlwind of confusion when she looked up at him. "You don't think I would simply take you on the ground, do you?"

"I didn't know…I mean I didn't think…" Thena scooted back on the bed, her dress balled up around her waist, and her long slender legs, full breasts, and dark caramel skin an enticing dish.

Priapus stripped off his shirt, barely able to take his eyes off her. She was hesitating. And he wouldn't force her. But there'd been a reason he'd been attracted to her, unable to leave her alone from the first second he'd caught sight of her. Looking down at her flushed expression, her gaze darting from him and then around her at the bed, he knew there was no way he would let her go without a fight. No woman had ever intrigued him as much as Thena did. Even now, hesitation so obvious in her expression, her curiosity warred within her. There was no fear. He sensed nothing hostile, just her indecisiveness as to whether she was doing the right thing or not. Well, he would damn well convince her this was the right thing.

He reached for his pants, grabbing her attention. When her tongue darted over her lips, the pain that rushed through his cock made it almost impossible to move. There weren't enough powers in his entire being to control the urge that pumped through him, an ache so intense that he doubted fucking her just once would relieve it.

Somehow he managed to loosen his pants and slide them down his legs.

"Priapus," Thena gasped, pulling her legs up to her chest as she inched away from him toward the other side of the bed.

Never in her life had she seen a cock so large. There was no way that would fit inside her, or any woman.

Chapter Nine

"You aren't fucking me with that." Thena went up on her knees, fighting to adjust her dress that refused to untangle around her waist.

She wouldn't deny that the most magnificent man she'd ever laid eyes on stood before her. The perfect sprinkling of brown hair dusted over his muscular chest and arms. His stomach was flat and firm. He had an abdomen to die for. So tall and well-proportioned, she wouldn't argue for a moment that he was definitely a god.

She ached for him. Her insides throbbing like one giant exposed nerve ending. And up until a minute ago, the only fear consuming her was that they were outside, exposed to anyone who might come upon them. Not that that would be too likely out in the middle of nowhere.

She'd admitted a bit of hesitation about letting him fuck her. They were practically strangers. Other than the fact that he seemed to be everywhere she was, and always there when she needed him, she didn't know that much about him. And it wasn't her style to just jump in the sack with a man. Which more than likely was the reason why her body cried out to have him so desperately.

But now, looking at his cock which was as thick as her arm, and as long as her forearm, throbbing out in front of him... Swollen and ready, it was a weapon she knew she couldn't take on.

"You're too big," she murmured, more than aware of the disappointment that rushed through her.

Priapus smiled. A man never tired of hearing those words. Kneeling next to her on the bed, he cupped her face with his hands, ensuring she would only look at his face.

"I promise you that I won't hurt you." He kissed her gently, soothing her, running his hands down her body and pressing her to him.

His cock pressed into the soft skin of her belly, his cock head touching the underside of her breasts. He would explode like a schoolboy if he didn't have her soon. But she needed time. He would have to prepare her, make her juices flow until she begged for him to be inside her.

Holding her to him, he adjusted her until she lay on the bed, the soft pillows surrounding her, adding elegance to beauty.

"I've got to taste you." He kissed first one nipple and then the other, while she arched into him, letting out a cry that added fever to his overwrought brain.

All Thena could do was hold on. This man, this god, worked over every one of her senses with his tongue. Creating a moist path down her belly, his hands caressed her, sending goose bumps rushing over her. She gripped his shoulders, feeling the corded muscles bulge underneath his smooth flesh. His skin was smooth, warm, and pulled taut over the most perfect body she'd ever seen.

She bucked, every muscle in her body tightening when he ran his tongue over the sensitive flesh between her legs.

"Dear God!" she cried out, digging her fingers into his flesh, wanting to push him away and hold him in place all at the same time.

She ran her fingers through his hair. It was so soft, and tickled her inner thighs. With the magic he worked on her pussy right now, taking time to get to know this man might be worth every minute. At the same time, she couldn't believe the craving she had to know him better. He was such a mystery, yet enticed her at the same time.

And with what he was doing to her right now…

Priapus growled, taking her legs and spreading her open. The soft pink flesh that appeared before him was a feast to a starving man. Slowly he ran his tongue over her creases, relishing her sweet taste. She was more than nectar to this god.

When he thrust inside her, tasting her cream as it flowed from her, he thought she would come off of the bed, her fingers pinching his shoulders while she cried out. Her cum spread over his face. He could drown in her and be an incredibly happy man.

"Shit!" She couldn't stand it another minute.

He devoured her cunt, lapping at her as if he hadn't had a meal in ages, and she was the main dish.

She would die, absolutely explode into a million pieces and never recover. Seldom had a man done this to her, ravished her with his mouth, fucked her with his tongue, brought her to such a quick orgasm with such little effort.

"You taste better than I imagined," he groaned, his breath hot against her skin.

"That feels so damned good," she whispered, feeling her orgasm build. "Please don't stop."

He moved his fingers, sliding two of them inside her while teasing her clit with his tongue. Feeling her insides clamp around him, her heat rush through him, his insides hardened knowing she would come for him.

"That's it, baby," he murmured, watching his fingers slide through her moist heat.

White cream soaked his fingers making it incredibly painful to just lie there and watch when his cock ached to sink deep into her heat.

"Priapus. I can't stand it." She bucked against his fingers, taking over and riding his hand while she dug her fingers into his hair. "Oh my God!"

Nerve endings exploded throughout her while she clamped down on his fingers, riding out her orgasm and holding onto his head. She didn't want him to stop what he was doing but knew if he continued she would pass out for sure. Wave after wave of passion rippled through her, yet she wanted more, so much more.

And he had it to offer.

That brought her pause, and she looked down at him, her body glistening with moisture while her breathing still came in heavy pants.

His green eyes glowed with a carnal satisfaction, that look of manly contentment knowing he had brought her to the point where she was now. On the edge, needing more, and knowing he was the one who had it.

She ran her tongue over her lips, letting her gaze fall to his massive cock, hardened to stone and extending a good foot out in front of him.

Was there a spell that would allow her to handle all of that?

"Let's see how much you can handle," he told her, moving her legs so that he knelt between them, and looking down while his cock throbbed between her legs.

"There's no way..." She stopped when he began entering her, looking down and watching that massive cock glide into her pussy. "Oh God. Oh shit."

She gripped the pillows around her, but they were no solace. His cock continued to move inside her, slowly, filling her, spreading her, consuming her as if he would take over her entire body with it.

She was being filled by a god. Her insides swelled, greeting him, absorbing him inside her. And still he offered more.

Her muscles stretched, while he continued to glide deeper. There was no way she would be able to handle this. Already the buildup of pressure was enough to make her want to scream. She clamped down on her mouth, more than aware that they were outside, quite a distance from everyone, but still...

"You are so hot, Thena. Damn, woman." Priapus arched his back, closing his eyes and letting his head fall back while enjoying her moist heat surrounding his shaft.

She'd not taken even half of him, and although it entered his mind to adjust their bodies, allow both of them to experience the full benefits he could offer, he wanted to experience Thena as she was. There would be no powers used, not this first time at least.

The pressure was getting too intense. She would pass out, or die, or explode or something. Thena fought to breathe, his cock impaling her, separating her entire insides. The pressure inside her seemed to implode, seeping around his cock while he filled her with a cock no human should be allowed to possess.

But then, he wasn't human, was he?

She couldn't think, couldn't move. Her body shivered, an orgasm tearing through her like she'd never experienced before.

Wave after wave rushed through her. Never had a cock this size been in her before. Hell, at the moment she couldn't even remember the last time she'd had sex. Priapus was rearranging her insides. She just knew it. She couldn't breathe, could no longer think, and she was damn sure if he continued she would pass out. Fade into blackness. Miss out on what might be the best time of her life.

When she was about to cry out, beg him not to fill her any more, he began pulling out, slowly, caressing her feverish insides with his too-large cock.

"Thena," he whispered. "Look at me."

More than anything he wanted to see the pleasure in her eyes, in her expression, while he fucked her.

She had to think to open her eyes, and then focus on those deep green eyes, glazed over and staring down at her with more compassion than she'd expected to see.

Every muscle in his body was taut, rippling under such perfectly smooth skin. His arms held him over her, triceps and biceps bulging. The spray of hair covering his chest glistened with moisture while his body filled her vision above her. His expression was too intense, too controlled. He fought to not hurt her, was holding back. She sensed that and wanted to reach out, help ease his pain. But she knew she didn't have what it took to give him what he truly needed.

He was just too damned big.

"You can handle me," he told her, knowing her thoughts. She ached for his happiness and that filled him with a warmth he hadn't expected.

Her concern to please him made his cock swell even more. She sucked in a breath, feeling him, enjoying him. He could tell by the look on her face. There was no pain, no regret, only the intense ache to give him the pleasure that he was giving her. If she only knew how damned good she felt.

"Not…fair." She could hardly speak. But this mind reading thing was going to come to a halt.

And she would tell him as much, if he weren't driving her into a complete frenzy as he retreated out of her, only to begin entering her again.

"Oh…shit."

This time he filled her faster, building the momentum, taking her over the edge with him once again. She dared to look down between them, see his massive cock disappear almost halfway inside her, then two-thirds, before pulling out and then plummeting in again.

His expression hardened, a flush covering his face while his body hardened over hers. The scent of their lovemaking filled her nostrils, and she dared to reach up, run her fingers up his arms, feel the strength that filled her while he moved faster and harder.

His heart pounded against her palms when she ran her hands over his chest. Her inner thigh muscles stretched while she pulled up her legs, wrapping them around him. Suddenly she wanted to feel him with every part of her body. The heat growing between the two of them was extraordinary. He pounded her soft flesh, reaching deeper inside her than anyone ever had before.

Her orgasm peaked again, white lights sparkling before her eyes as she came. "Priapus!" She screamed his name, no longer able to hold back.

When she was sure she would pass out, no longer be able to handle the fucking he was giving her, he seemed to grow even more inside her.

"My turn, baby," he said through gritted teeth, and white heat shattered inside her.

Nothing could compare. Never had she had an experience such as this. And she would be damned lucky if she lived to be able to tell about it. Her insides burned from muscles never used, and orgasms more intense than she ever thought possible.

She went limp underneath him, wishing she could cuddle into the large bed and simply sleep for a while.

But even as her body tingled from the intense pleasure she'd just experienced, her mind began churning with the many incidents that had just occurred.

The words from Maxine right before they'd left the gas station. Little Nate, who'd had so much evil in him it still made her skin crawl thinking about it. And then her mother announcing she had a father, a father who hadn't had the time to make an appearance in her life up until today.

And mixed up with all of that was Priapus, who lay next to her, his incredibly large cock damp, and resting against his abdomen clear up to his belly button while he stared up at the sky.

She ventured sitting, running her hands over her hair while she looked absently around them. Suddenly it seemed ridiculous to be lying on such a fancy bed out in the middle of a field. She was open-minded, probably more so than most. But all of this was getting to be too much.

It hurt to stand, her muscles in her inner thighs having received a better workout than she'd had in ages. How sad. To think that thirty minutes of a good time could render her tired and sore. Then she glanced down at Priapus, who appeared quite comfortable lying naked on the bed, his hands clasped behind his head.

One look was all the realization she needed to understand why she felt every muscle in her body. Even sated, his cock was way too large. Granted, he looked damn good lying there—sexy as hell, in fact.

"Your task ahead of you won't be easy." He didn't look at her right away, but continued to stare at the sky, those soft green eyes the only part of his expression appearing alert.

"My task?" She fought with her dress, managing to untangle it from her waist and readjust it on her body.

"You aren't a witch, Thena. You're a goddess." Priapus looked her way, catching a quick glance at her full ripe breasts before she covered them with her dress. "You will have to learn the extent of your powers. That task will take time."

"I've been doing that all my life." She wouldn't let him see how his words twisted her tummy into knots. "There is no proof that man back there is my father."

Priapus leaned on his elbow, turning to his side and giving her his full attention. "He is your father."

She couldn't look away. Her mouth went dry while she lost herself for a moment in the sensual gaze he bestowed on her. But it was more than that. There was an intelligence, a vast amount of knowledge that terrified her for a moment. Somehow she *knew* he spoke the truth, although she wished she could claim it was otherwise.

"I see," she said, running her tongue over her lips to moisten them.

Her heart raced in her chest, and simply staring at his naked body made it hard to stay focused. She turned from him, staring back in the direction of town. Slowly she moved off the bed, standing on wobbly legs she feared for a moment wouldn't hold her. Her entire body pulsed with the fucking she'd just received.

Blowing out a breath of determination, she worked to untwist her dress and put herself back together.

"Once I've had a chance to speak further with Triton, I will understand why you've been kept in the dark about your heritage." Priapus suddenly stood behind her, his strong fingers pressing into her shoulders.

Thena turned around quickly. "No." She pointed a finger at his face. "Don't you dare go speaking to that man."

Priapus took her hand in his, pulling her finger to his mouth. He loved how her eyes turned a dark chocolate color when her passions flared.

"I can understand him better than you can," he tried to explain. "We'll have answers so much sooner. And in the meantime, we can work to help you learn your powers."

"I need to do this by myself." She spoke quietly, not wishing to offend him, but in no way wanting him prying into matters that were so personal, matters that she didn't even understand herself.

Priapus smiled, her free spirit making her even more enticing. "There is plenty you will be able to do yourself. But you need protection."

"If I hear that one more time today," she blurted out, throwing her hands up in the air and turning away from him. "I'm thirty years old and have done pretty damned good for myself so far."

She turned around, frustration fueling anger inside her. "And who's to say that I don't need protection from you?"

She regretted the words as soon as she'd said them. In her heart she knew that Priapus would never hurt her, not intentionally anyway. What she really needed was protection from herself, from her heart, from being hurt if she dared to care for this man too much.

Priapus' smile faded when something gripped at his gut that he didn't take time to identify. There was no way he could let her take all of this on by herself. He stepped into her, watching her expression harden, her emotions raging through her although she battled to keep them under control. All that she managed was maintaining the glare that she graced him with. He ignored it, wrapping a strand of her coarse black hair between two fingers.

"There are demons stalking this planet. You've cast one of them out, grabbed their attention, and they will come after you." He spoke slowly, not wishing to frighten her, but knowing a bit of the truth would help her to see the seriousness of the matter. "You need me. And I have no intention of walking away from you."

He barely had time to read her fury before she slapped his hand away from her hair. "Don't you think for a moment you can have sex with me, and then assume I'm yours to tell what to do. I do not need you!"

His words had more than outraged her. They had terrified her.

Demons! What the fuck did he mean by demons?

If one more bit of information got put in her head today, she would explode, absolutely explode. She turned from him again, this time storming off across the field. Ignoring him when he called after her, she began walking with as much determination as the sore muscles throughout her body would allow.

Chapter Ten

Priapus had half a mind to show her how much she did need him. He watched her walk across the field, her tight ass swaying deliciously in her dress. At the rate she was going, it would be dark before she managed to walk back to town. Not to mention she was an open invitation for too many demons to come after her.

It was time to do some serious convincing.

Flying after her, he lifted her into his arms with little effort. "I don't take kindly to being walked out on," he whispered in her ear as he pulled her to him.

Thena thought her heart would explode. Her feet left the ground so fast, she barely had time to register anything other than the hard body that suddenly pressed against her. Strong, sturdy arms wrapped around her, making it hard to move. The way his breath tortured the side of her face sent a vicious wave of lust rushing through her.

But she wouldn't let him own her. With the amount of powers he had, she'd have no life at this rate. All of her life she'd worked alone, keeping others at bay so she wouldn't be hurt. No one had ever manipulated her, or told her what to do. She'd lived her life knowing she was an outcast, a black witch, accepted by some but for the most part shunned. If she let him into her heart, he would control her every move and that wasn't going to happen. She twisted furiously in his arms, realizing she was holding on to him for dear life, and at the same time wanting to clobber him.

She had no idea what she was capable of doing—if she could perform any stunts at all compared to him. But it was damn sure time to find out.

"You will not control me," she hissed, forcing her thoughts to focus on making them stop flying through the air, instead of his perfect body that held her way too close.

The two of them came to a stop, hovering a foot or so above the ground.

"You're accustomed to incantations, spells," he told her calmly, still holding her in his arms, hard solid muscle bulging against her everywhere. "You don't need to speak your powers. Simply will the elements around you. They will respond."

"Fine." She imagined him taking a punch to the gut.

"Well, hells," he grumbled, doubling over and at the same time letting her go.

Thena fell to the ground, and not too lightly.

Her bare knees and palms burned instantly when she hit the hard field of grass and dirt. She fought the tears of pain that quickly burned her eyes.

I just want to be home, she thought miserably, embarrassment and anger making her feel sick to her stomach. She'd never hit another person in her life, not in anger, not playfully. And she'd sure never used her magic to cause someone else pain.

Ever mind the rule of three; what you send comes back to thee. Her mother's words sang through her head, a lesson she'd been taught at such a young age. *If you intentionally bring harm to another person, that harm will come back to you with three times the strength.* Even as she knelt there, she could see the seriousness in her mother's expression in her mind as she explained how not to use her magic. Never intentionally harm someone else. A simple rule she'd just broken. She'd disregarded the *Threefold of Karma.*

Priapus floated to the ground slowly, standing over her, but making no attempt to touch her or help her up. He'd keep in mind for future reference that she had a nasty temper. He'd never hit a lady in his entire existence, and had no desire to start now.

"Let me know when you've calmed down," he told her, watching while she knelt on all fours looking at the ground.

"I shouldn't have done that and I'm sorry," she said quietly, not looking up at him.

"Does that mean you're calm now?"

"No." And she wasn't. At that moment, she doubted if she would ever be calm again.

"Thena. Stand up." He itched to reach out and help her up, to once again feel her pressed against him.

So beautiful and so stubborn. Damn it if she wasn't making him hard all over again. Glancing around the quiet field, he fought for solace with his thoughts. She shouldn't be getting to him like this, yet she was.

"Don't tell me what to do."

"Would you stand up, Thena, please?" He fisted his hands, fighting the urge to make her stand, make her see the peril that surrounded her, make her realize she needed him. And damn it if he didn't want to take care of her.

Thena huffed out a breath of air. Her hands burned. Standing, she brushed dirt and grass from her dress, knowing there was no way she could meet his gaze at the moment.

His tone had been gentle though, softening the outer edges of her frustration. She doubted there was anything he could do to ease her embarrassment. And she knew that no powers could possibly exist that would calm her racing heart. She didn't know what to expect when she returned home. She didn't know how to feel about this man who'd turned her insides to jelly in such a short time. And she sure as hell didn't have a clue about these damned demons he'd mentioned.

"I just want to go home. I need a shower." She did her best to look composed in front of him.

But there wasn't a bit of doubt in her mind that she looked like shit at the moment.

"Then will yourself home," Priapus encouraged.

She looked up at him, her expression doubtful. He couldn't keep his hands off her any longer. Reaching for a strand of hair that bordered her face, he brushed it back. Her hair was like coarse silk, contrasting with her smooth warm skin.

She looked away from him briefly, her thick black lashes bordering brown eyes that filled with so many emotions. In that small moment of time, he could drown in her, the intensity of her soul unending. He sensed so much power, so raw and untamed. The urge to reach inside her and scoop up all of her sensuality, her fears, her excitement for the unknown, all of those emotions and wrap himself into them and soothe her made the protector in him come to life with a vengeance.

But before he could speak, Thena closed her eyes. "It's time to go home now."

Priapus was actually surprised when she disappeared right in front of him.

But not as surprised as Thena was when suddenly she stood in her bedroom and no longer in the field she'd been in a moment before.

"Holy shit." She took a step or two backwards, her heart suddenly pounding so hard that she couldn't catch her breath. "That didn't just happen."

For a moment she thought she might fall over, her footing unsteady. The sensation that she'd just run real fast and stopped just as quickly had her reaching out to stabilize herself.

If she had powers like that she would have known before now. Had she really just pulled off such an unbelievable feat?

She stared around the room, searching for answers to questions she couldn't even voice. None of this made any sense. She was almost panting. Reaching for her heart, she turned around in her room, still unable to believe she was standing here.

"What kind of magic is this?" she asked her quiet bedroom, and obviously got no answer.

Her simple bedroom, the one she'd grown up in, had cried and laughed and shared secrets with long-lost friends in, comforted her with its familiar surroundings. Her mother hadn't changed much about it over the years she'd been gone. It was almost as if, somehow, her mom had known she could come back.

She moved over to the single bed, with its left bottom leg probably still marking the loose floorboard underneath it, where she'd hidden her most valuable possessions.

The bed was still firm, and she sat on it for a moment, slowing her breath, letting the safety of her room engulf her. There was her dresser, with the second drawer down that had the fake back. She remembered the painstaking hours it had taken, while her mother was at work and she left home alone, to insert the false back so she would have a private space where she could store items that no one else would see.

Alone. She had spent so many hours alone in this room. And why? Because her mother had worked so many long hours trying to support the two of them. That hadn't been easy for a black woman to do twenty or so years ago. Hell—it wasn't easy now. And they'd been alone because there had been no man who stepped forward and claimed her as his daughter.

She looked toward her bedroom door, her heart hardening as she wondered where her mother might be—where that man was who suddenly had appeared in her life.

Triton. His name was Triton. And Priapus seemed convinced that he was her father. She rubbed her face with her hands, knowing she needed to shower, still feeling the aftermath of having had such intense sex. Maybe just a bit of this would make more sense if she freshened up a bit. Clean the body, and clean the mind.

The phone rang downstairs and she heard her mother answer it. Her mom's soft voice was such a familiar sound, as was everything about this house. Strange things were happening, and they would control her, only if she let them.

"And I can't let that happen," she said, with determination.

The front door opened downstairs, there were voices, and then it shut, leaving her in the familiar silence of an empty house. She'd figure out where her mother went soon, first she needed to shower.

Plenty of soap and clean clothes didn't help her as much as she wished they would. She tingled from head to toe, still feeling everywhere Priapus had touched her. Her insides were tender yet she craved more of him. It must have something to do with having gone so long without. Her juices had been turned on and now they were going full force.

Her mother hadn't left a note, or given any indication of where she'd gone. Everything seemed in place.

Uneasiness ran through her though. "And if only I could place why I feel this way," she mumbled.

Thoughts of talking to her Gramma, sitting cuddled next to her on the couch downstairs just as she had many times as a child, suddenly appealed to her. Gramma always had a way of making sense out of things. Even when she didn't know how to sort into words what bothered her, Gramma had a way of understanding, of putting things in proper perspective.

"This one might be too big even for you, Gramma," she conceded with a sigh.

Somehow she had to sort through this on her own. She'd taken care of herself for years, and she wouldn't stop now. When things got a bit too sticky, she'd always resorted to the comfort of her surroundings, and her magic.

Even though she'd grown up here, too many years had passed for her to feel this was her home. She'd brought her personal supplies with her, packed safely in her suitcase, so that she could perform any incantations or spells needed.

"Could I actually do magic without them?" She'd never fathomed the thought.

But after everything that happened today, she was starting to have a few new thoughts. One of them being the intense desire to explore what might have been inside of her all along.

She paced from the kitchen into the living room, staring at the front door briefly while the urge to leave and go find her mother surged through her.

"She's probably out looking for me." And suddenly she felt bad for running out on her.

They needed to talk, sort through this newfound knowledge of her father.

"I wonder where he went." But she didn't want to know. She wasn't ready to see him again, not yet. "No. I want to know where Mom is."

And she began pacing again, frowning while she thought of possible places her mother might be.

She tugged on the plain T-shirt she'd donned, fidgeting with the material as she closed her eyes, imagining her mother driving into town.

"Wherever you be, appear for me," she whispered, no longer pacing but standing in the middle of her mom's living room.

Her heart beat silently against her ribs, while she slowed her breath, keeping her mind focused on her mother's face.

"Wherever you be, appear for me," she repeated, relaxing the muscles throughout her body.

She repeated her plea one more time, her body completely relaxed now, her thoughts focused on her mother.

A strange urgency rushed over her, emotions that didn't feel like her own. She was sensing her mother's thoughts and she grasped them eagerly, wrapping her own thoughts around them. But where was she?

Her body slowly levitated, like it often did when she cast her spells. But focusing on keeping her feet on the ground would distract her from her mother. And she didn't like the feelings that were coming over her.

Wherever her mother had gone, she was worried, concerned about something.

Thena squeezed her eyes shut so hard they hurt, but she wouldn't do anything to ease her own body. All of her attention had to remain on her mom, or she would lose the connection she'd created.

Where are you? She needed to see around her mother, create a bigger picture in her mind to help her figure out where her mother had gone. Suddenly the sensation that she was gripping something really hard made her hands hurt. A view of town flashed in front of her, the road, the glare of the sun.

An unpleasant sensation rippled through her—fear, something evil.

Her mother was in trouble!

That simple knowledge hit her so hard that she opened her eyes, suddenly gasping for breath as she fell to the ground—for the third time that day. Her tennis shoes eased her landing on her mother's carpeted floor.

"I've got to find a way to get to her," she said, looking around her quickly at her quiet surroundings.

The image she'd just seen in her mind was fading. But she knew that for a brief moment, she'd seen through her mother's eyes. Thena fought to hold the image, place where in town her Mom had been. Margaret had been gripping her steering wheel. Thena could still feel its hardness against her palms. And she was in town. Thena had seen the grocery store. At least that's what she thought.

The mental picture faded, and she slapped her hands to her temples, fighting to hold on to it, desperately needing to focus on where her mother was so possibly she could guess where she was heading.

If only her mother carried a cellular phone.

Thena had no car. And she still had no clue exactly where her mother was.

Aggravation rippled through her. She hated feeling helpless.

Priapus.

He would be able to help her. She thought of calling out for him, curious if he would simply appear before her. Someone knocked on her door, the intrusion of sound almost making her heart explode when it skipped a beat.

She hurried to open it, ready to tell Priapus that she needed to find her mother.

Tommy Joe Baker stood in front of her, his hand lifted ready to knock again.

Sunlight drifted in around her when she opened the door, but she didn't feel it. A cold chill swallowed the warmth as she stared into his dark brooding gaze.

Tall and thin, he towered over her, but his gaunt frame barely blocked the sunlight behind him. A wide black belt held his worn blue jeans to his waist, while a white T-shirt clung to his narrow frame. He had the sleeves rolled up to his shoulders, making his long arms almost look skeletal. In ten years, he hadn't changed much in appearance.

"Had a feeling I'd be able to catch you alone here," he drawled.

She caught a glimpse of his pickup truck pulled in sideways in the driveway, the front tires sinking deep into the soft ground of her mama's front yard. Tommy Joe reached for the screen door, pulling it open while a slow sneer appeared on his face.

"What you come back to Barren for?" he asked, his mouth barely moving when he talked.

Something was definitely different about his manner though. Tommy Joe had always been awkward, a bit on the shy side—far from good-looking, he'd never been in with the cool kids or athletes. But he'd always been friendly, seeking her out, willing to do whatever she wanted. Harmless and sweet were the simplest words to describe him.

At the moment, his aura suggested quite the opposite.

He still wasn't good-looking, but his shyness seemed to have left him. Determination saturated the space between them. His washed-out blue eyes seemed cold and distant. The insecure boy was gone. Something hard and mean had taken over.

She didn't want to step backward to allow him into the home. But holding her ground would have put them way too close to each other.

"I was just leaving," she told him, immediately aware of a foul stench that surrounded him.

It turned her stomach. She crossed her arms, confused that he seemed so cold-hearted. Tommy Joe had always been a friendly sort, nothing like his old man who'd always been an asshole.

"You fixin' to take a walk? Or were you going to fly out of here? How were you going to leave, Thena? It's quite a hike into town." When he looked down at her, she saw the hatred, the swarming evil that put all the cruelty his father had ever shown to shame.

"Tommy Joe, you get out of here." Nothing about him intimidated her. She wouldn't let it. "It's none of your business where I'm going, or how I get there."

"I don't think you're going anywhere." He reached for her, his dirty fingernails grabbing her attention when he tried to touch her face.

Outrage. Fury. Anger so intense that it clogged her senses rushed out of him.

"What's gotten into you, Tommy Joe?" She tried to make a show out of her confusion, frantically biding time while she tried to figure out what to do. "We were always friends, I thought. You come back later and we'll have a soda, catch up on old times."

He reached for her again, this time grabbing her arm. His icy fingers chilled her to the bone. Looking up, she saw it—the same evil that had harbored in little Nate.

What the hell was going on here?

There is evil lurking everywhere. Her Mom sure hadn't lied about that.

"Who are you?" she asked before she could stop herself.

"You just said we were always friends, and now you ask who I am?" Tommy Joe's laugh curdled her blood.

She glared at him, trying to yank her arm away but he held on fast, moving in closer and forcing her to back up until they stood in the middle of the living room.

"I don't have time for games." She stared at her arm where he held on with icy cold long fingers. "Let go of my arm."

"Believe me, Miss Thena. This ain't no game." Tommy Joe yanked on her arm, causing her almost to fall into him.

"Let go of me!" Thena pulled back as hard as she could, surprised when she couldn't sway Tommy Joe. "I don't know what you've done to Tommy Joe, but you need to get the hell out of here—and now!"

He was a lot stronger than he looked.

"You aren't wanted here," he hissed, his voice sounding almost too deep. "This is your only warning to get out of town. Do you understand me?"

No. She didn't understand any of this. But she was beginning to see that something was possessing the people of Barren, Kentucky. Some type of evil harbored within these people. No wonder her mother had wanted her to come home.

Tommy Joe had always had a puppy-dog personality, a sheepish grin on his face. She'd been forbidden fruit to him, his daddy not approving of her. He'd never judged her for her race though, and she never thought less of him for coming from a line of bigots. They had been friends. She wouldn't have dated him even if his daddy had approved. But she'd never disliked him.

The man who held her arm in a vise grip right now wasn't Tommy Joe Baker. He might look like him. It was Tommy Joe on the outside. But whoever, or whatever, existed inside his body, was evil and disgusting.

"I'll stay here as long as I damn well please." She was getting sick and tired of being manhandled.

She glared at his hand, which was beginning to cut the circulation off in her arm.

"I don't think you understand," he sneered, his voice seeming to echo in the living room.

"No. I don't think *you* understand." A memory hit her, something she and Tommy Joe had shared in the past.

A trick…nothing fancy…just something she'd learned how to do at an early age. She'd showed the other children and they'd laughed at her, teased and despised her for being different. Everyone but Tommy Joe. He'd been fascinated, and had asked her to do it again and again.

The memory that hit her was when she was no more than ten at the oldest. She and Tommy Joe had been in the field out back, and she'd been able to set blades of grass on fire with her finger. It had been so simple. The other kids had run off, calling her weird, the daughter of a witch, making her feel silly that she'd shown them her trick. But Tommy Joe had been impressed. And they'd spent the rest of the afternoon starting small fires and putting them out quickly so they wouldn't get discovered.

She stared at Tommy Joe's hand, his long fingers wrapped around her arm. "Remember the fires I used to start, Tommy Joe?" she asked, hoping to put enough mystery in her tone to feed his worry. "I could start fires with a finger. Maybe I could start a fire with your fingers."

"What?" he stammered, and his grip lightened.

Whatever consumed Tommy Joe had access to his memories. She could sense it. The evil that lurked around him changed to fear, worry, suspicion.

"You remember. With just a thought...poof! There was the fire." She didn't take her gaze off his fingers, her mind working, her thoughts focused on burning his fingers.

She felt the heat in her arm at the same time that Tommy Joe let go of her, yelping loudly like a beaten pup.

There wasn't much time. She couldn't let his fear subside, but instead needed to work off of it, take the upper hand.

"If you don't get the hell out of here right now, I'll burn your entire body. Don't think I can't do it. Lighting a finger on fire was child's play. And I'm not a child anymore." She'd never lit anything on fire since those childhood days, but she'd be damned if she would let Tommy Joe know that.

He took a step backward, his eyes bulging open so wide for a moment they looked like they would pop right out of his head.

"I'm not done with you," he hissed, pointing a long skinny finger at her as he backed to the door. "Show your strength. In the end, it will be your downfall. We are much stronger than you ever will be."

And with that he backed out of her door, letting the screen door slam closed behind him.

She stood there for a minute, shaking and trying to understand what he'd meant by his words. *We* are much stronger. *Who the hell are "we"?*

There wasn't time to stand there and ponder his words. She hurried to the door in time to see him hop into his truck, mumbling something she couldn't catch before pulling his truck door closed and firing the engine to life.

"May your truck break down on the way into town," she muttered, wishing him good riddance and bad luck.

Before closing the door and locking it, she looked around the yard, curious to where Priapus had disappeared. It almost surprised her that he hadn't run to her rescue.

"But I didn't need him." She'd handled the matter nicely all by herself.

And although she had half a mind to rush outside, make sure that Tommy Joe had left, she needed to focus on where her mother was. A sinking feeling in her gut told her that her mother might be in trouble.

Chapter Eleven

Her mother had a book of spells. And regardless of the fact that Priapus had told her that she didn't need to use incantations or props to work magic, it was the life she knew.

"Old habits just die hard," she said out loud, speaking to Priapus even though she didn't sense him anywhere nearby.

Maybe he'd achieved his goal with her. Now that he had his piece of ass he wouldn't be around as much. Wasn't that just like a man?

Well, she didn't need him anyway. She'd gotten rid of Tommy Joe Baker all by herself. Now she would find her mother, and figure out how to get to her.

Priapus had given her the time of her life. She wouldn't deny that. Never in her wildest dreams had she imagined a cock that size. He'd left her so satisfied, yet already she fantasized about doing him again. There were other positions, a variety of ways to satisfy each other.

Thinking about all of that right now wouldn't help her accomplish a thing. She didn't need a man in her life anyway.

Nonetheless, she let out a deep sigh, fighting off the uncomfortable settling in her tummy, and focused on figuring out what to do about her mother. In spite of the thoughts she kept having about Priapus, the worry that her mother needed her was becoming more than a distraction.

Her mother always kept her book of spells on a shelf she'd put up in their living room. "We'll call it our mantelpiece," Margaret had teased so many years ago.

Thena still remembered the satisfied smile her mother had on her face with hammer still in hand after they'd successfully mounted the shelf on the living room wall.

"If we did have a fireplace, it would look best in this wall, don't you think?" Her mother had always inspired the use of imagination.

And Thena had agreed. She hurried over to the shelf, remembering how she'd pretended there had been a fireplace in that wall for years after that shelf had gone up. There had been days when she swore she could feel the heat and hear the crackling wood when she sat on the living room floor and played.

The book of spells rested on the shelf, next to a bowl of fresh herbs. Not a spot of dust lay on the shelf. Her mother still used the book often, its worn pages proof of the attention it got.

She took the book into the kitchen and flipped through the pages carefully, not wanting to accidentally tear the fragile paper.

"A spell to find someone…there you are." She ran her finger over several of them, opting not to use any that required blood.

She'd never been into poking herself, or inflicting pain just to get results. Her finger stopped over a directional spell.

The power of the book seeped through her finger as she stroked the page. She could feel the warmth, the strength from her mother as a result of so many successful spells pulled from these pages.

"All I need are compass candles." She'd become an expert on learning what type of candles worked best for what spells.

She hurried to the cabinet in the dining room where numerous candles had always been kept, intent on her task, and ignoring the small voice deep inside her that suggested she might be able to find her mother without a spell. There wasn't time to dabble with the unknown. It was best to stick to what she knew how to do. Pulling open the wooden door, which was actually part of a very old kitchen cabinet where most of the family heirlooms were kept, she hurried through the stacks of candles until she found what she was looking for.

The wax of this particular candle, the compass candle, burned quickly, dripping heavily, which was what she needed for her spell.

She looked down at the half-full box of matches and smiled. "Candle, you don't need matches to light, do you?"

The candle burst into flame, building her confidence that she would soon find out where her mother went. She might not be a goddess like Priapus had suggested, but she was a damn good witch.

Placing the candle in a candleholder on the kitchen table she relaxed her mind, worked to release the anxiety that had built up inside her while Tommy Joe had been here. No longer would she dwell on Priapus, or where he might be. This wasn't the time to think about the incredible sex she'd had on a magical bed in the middle of a field. All she would do right now is focus on where her mother was.

"You are to the north," she said, guiding her hands over the flame, directing it to the north. "And you are to the south," she said, pulling her hands back to her belly while she stood over the burning candle. "You are to the west. And you are to the east."

She moved her hands over the flame in each direction, closing her eyes, feeling the heat of the small flame dance under her skin.

"Burn the wax. Let it drip. Show me the direction in town where my mother went." She directed the candle, telling it what she wanted to know.

Her mother's emotions grew stronger inside of her. She could smell the sweet smell that was unique to her mom, a mixture of soap and hair grease, along with a faint dab of perfume. It was as if she stood next to her mom, even though they weren't together. Worry and fear clamored around her mom. Whatever her mother was doing, she wasn't sure about it. There was hesitation too. A strong urgency rushed through her that her mother really needed help.

Others stood around her mother. Thena sensed she was no longer driving, but at her destination. Images fogged in her mind, a room, someone's home maybe.

Opening her eyes, she stared at the candle, which had notably burnt to the left, the wax dripping down that side of the candle. To her left was the west. Her mother was on the west side of town.

Thena smiled. "Thank you, compass candle, for showing me the way."

She blew out the candle, and focused on her next challenge.

The only transportation she had was her feet. Well, it wouldn't be the first time she'd walked from home into town. But as a child she'd viewed it as an adventure, always being able to take her mother's "charged with fresh magic" walking stick. Now it simply sounded like an incredibly slow means to get somewhere.

"What if I could just will myself to Mom?" she speculated, remembering how she'd come home from being in the field with Priapus.

But had she really done that on her own? It made more sense to think Priapus had sent her home, allowing her to believe she was more magical than she actually was. Although why he would do that she had no clue.

Well, if she was going anywhere, she needed to get ready to go. After a quick trip to the bathroom, smoothing down her hair with her scented hair grease, and dabbing just a bit of makeup on, she returned to the living room.

She would have to walk, she just knew it, and then more than likely ask around once she got into town, but there was no harm in trying to will herself to her mother.

"I want to go to my Mom," she said with her eyes closed. And she wasn't a bit surprised when she opened them and found herself standing in her living room still. "I knew it wouldn't work."

"And that's why it didn't," Priapus said from behind her, scaring the crap out of her.

"Holy shit!" She turned around quickly, grabbing her heart.

Priapus smiled at her, moving in and pulling her into his arms. "I didn't mean to scare you."

"Yeah, right."

More than likely he found it more than humorous. She looked up into those pale green eyes, dying to ask where he'd been. But she couldn't take time for that conversation. Right now she had other things to focus her attention on.

"Where are you going?" He ran his hands down her arm.

Her nipples hardened against her shirt while he watched, and he ran his hands over them, the hard nubs puckering further to greet his touch.

Thena sucked in a breath. Her breasts swelled, anxious for more attention, to be fondled and kissed. Damn it. She wanted him all over again and there wasn't time for this.

"I was headed out to join Mom." She made light of it, not wanting to give him the satisfaction of knowing she might need his help in finding her.

Priapus looked over her head, staring in the direction of the town while doing a quick search of the people who were there.

"She's over at Maxine Poller's house." He frowned, immediately sensing the increase in the demon's hostility.

He'd gone to seek out Triton, learn more of the details about the man's sudden appearance. The two of them hadn't had much to say to each other, and he hadn't been gone too long. But in the short absence, the demons had been sent into an uproar.

"What have you been doing while I was gone?" He returned his attention to her, immediately captivated by her soft brown eyes.

He ran his hands down her front, gripping her narrow waist. She'd been up to something and didn't want to talk to him about it. He frowned, trying harder to read her thoughts but too distracted by how pretty she looked.

She'd applied a bit of makeup, bringing out the soft curve of her cheekbones. Her full lips were moist and pursed like she would kiss him. Her long lashes fluttered over her eyes and she opened her mouth to answer him but then didn't say anything. For a moment she just stared at him, looking more beautiful than she had in his mind's image that he'd dwelt on ever since leaving her. He credited that to the glow of damn good sex.

He couldn't wait to fuck her again.

"I told you. I'm getting ready to leave." She pushed away from him, too quickly getting lost in her own desires the longer he held her pressed up against that virile body.

If she didn't get out of there soon, all of that hard muscle, the way he looked at her with his carnal gaze, would have her going limp in his arms, begging him to kiss her, to touch her the way he had earlier that day. And she wasn't sure her body could endure another round with him just yet. She still tingled all over from their lovemaking. And standing so close to him simply reminded her how much she'd enjoyed it.

"As you wish." Priapus backed away, a bemused expression on his face. "Don't let me stop you."

She stared at him oddly. After a second, she turned toward the door. At least now she knew where on the west side of Barren her mom was.

She looked over her shoulder, and then glared at him when he hadn't moved. "You can't stay here alone in my mother's house."

Now he was amused. He could enter and leave this home at will. "And my dear, where would you have me go?"

He moved toward her, looking down with his brooding gaze on fire. Domination and an unsettling edge of lust made his face hard. She swallowed with some effort. No way would she back down to him, or give in to such ridiculous questions.

"Don't mock me," she told him, opening the front door and then stepping to the side so that he could leave first. "You and I both know you'll go wherever you damn well please."

"How true." He pulled her into his arms, ignoring her gasping surprise, and kissed her protests away.

Lifting them, he willed the door to shut behind him as he moved them through space toward town.

Whether she realized at that moment what they were doing or not, she relaxed into him, deepening their kiss. Their tongues danced with enthusiasm, promising more passion and intense lovemaking. His groin hardened while he ran his hands down her back, cupping her rear end.

Thena's world spun around her. Priapus' hands were all over her, caressing, stroking her into a heated frenzy. She was spinning, like everything was moving too fast and at the same time standing still. Rock-hard muscles pressed against her everywhere.

For a moment she was sure her feet left the ground. But then she felt the hard surface underneath her again. If she began to float, holding on to Priapus must have kept her grounded.

She broke off the kiss, needing air. She was getting so lightheaded she would pass out if she didn't breathe soon.

Never had she been kissed like that before. Her eyes fluttered open, her vision blurred for a moment.

He looked down at her, his green eyes a deep passionate shade. But then she blinked, her senses slowly coming to her.

"What the hell?" She looked around, and then backed away from Priapus quickly. "Where am I?"

The first thing she noticed was her mother's car. Looking around quickly, it took a minute before she recognized Maxine Poller's home. She hadn't been here in years.

"I thought this is where you wanted to be." Priapus crossed his arms over his chest, his roped muscles moving distractingly in his arms.

Thena shook her head, amazed at his abilities and wanting to question him as to how the hell he managed it.

"Yes. And thank you." She turned toward the house, pausing when she realized there were several other cars parked in the driveway too.

If she only knew what was going on inside, what she was walking into. She'd been so anxious to get to her mother it hadn't crossed her mind that she might be an unwanted visitor.

Priapus came up behind her, gripping her shoulders with strong fingers. "Go on inside. Have faith in what you can do, and don't let anyone intimidate you. I'll be close by if you need me."

She looked up at him, surprised by his last comment. His face was so close, his expression serious yet relaxed. He knew what was going on in there, yet wasn't enlightening her. And as much as she wanted to ask questions, she simply nodded once, and headed toward the house.

Taking a deep breath, she knocked on the front door.

She didn't knock hard, just a tap with her knuckles. There was a large group inside, and they were busy doing something. She could sense it. Priapus' strength wrapped around her, yet when she glanced over her shoulder, he was gone.

The door opened and she turned her attention to Maxine, whose expression was a wave of excitement.

"Why Thena! How wonderful that you are here." The older woman's grin broadened, and she opened the door further, gesturing for her to enter. "Your powers will make this work for sure," she added under her breath.

Thena didn't question her but entered quietly, taking in the atmosphere in the room.

Almost a dozen women stood in a circle, turning to acknowledge her. She quickly noticed her mother among them. In the middle of the circle, bound to a chair and gagged, a man sat, glaring at her.

Chapter Twelve

"What's going on here?" Thena asked, taking in the familiar faces of women from town.

Brooms lay at each woman's feet, which formed a circle around the man tied to the chair. The women looked excited, anxious, determination etched on their faces.

Their energy filled the living room area. Furniture had been pushed back, out of the way, chairs stacked on the couch, and curtains drawn making the room dim. An overhead light beamed down on them, and numerous candles were lit, scattered from the tops of shelves to end tables, and placed haphazardly on the dining room table. They were candles of all shapes and sizes and a variety of colors and scents, as if quantity mattered more than quality in drawing in the desired effect.

"I knew you would come." Maxine clapped her hands together and then pressed them to her bosom. She broke out of the circle, grinning broadly. "I just knew you would know to be here."

Thena blinked, unsure what to say, and gave her mother a side look. Margaret also seemed relieved to see her daughter. There was hesitation in her mother's soft brown eyes though. The way the wrinkles increased around her mother's mouth when Thena stepped into the room was enough indication that she was worried. Whether it was about Thena, or what was going on in the room, Thena couldn't be sure.

"My son." Maxine grabbed Thena's arm, dragging her forward into the midst of anxiety that the women had spawned. "He's got the devil in him. And I know you can cure him. We all know what you did for little Nate."

Thena licked her lips while trepidation seeped through her, making her skin damp with sweat. The room wasn't warm. In fact the simple living area almost seemed chilly, and Thena suddenly ached for fresh air.

The women shifted, turning their attention to her. So many eyes needling through her with emotions plummeting out of each of them that it was like they attacked her even though they didn't move. They were pinned to the spot where they stood, forming their circle, creating a force with bodies that kept the negative energy contained. Belief in the ritual had given them strength.

Her mother had instilled that in them. Something she'd never accomplished back home in Kansas City. Or maybe she'd simply given up on the fight. But her mother had the respect of each woman in this room. She glanced again at Margaret, at her mom, at the woman who'd kept her father from her all these years. Whatever her reasons, she had to admit, her mother was a strong woman, a woman this community loved.

Taking in a deep breath, she attempted a smile at Maxine. "All I can do is try. I can't make you any promises."

She watched the man in the middle of the circle, his black eyes burning with fury and outrage. He struggled with his bonds, his long lanky body pulling against the chair, making it jump around the living room floor. Some of the women looked at him nervously, and then turned their attention back to her. Their expressions pleaded with her. It was obvious every one of them seemed to think that she could accomplish what they were trying to do. Just the sighs of relief, their bodies relaxing some as they looked her way.

Margaret raised her hands, speaking quietly to the group. "We have to maintain the circle, ladies. His evil can't leave what we've created. Believe, and we'll be able to help him."

"I heard what you did for Audry Simpson's boy." One of the women in the circle spoke up.

Several others muttered that they'd heard as well. The Barren grapevine hadn't diminished in strength over the years.

"Margaret, you let your daughter heal Randy. His own mother believes she can do it." Another one of the women spoke up.

Thena couldn't remember everyone's names but she recognized faces. The entire community of gossiping know-it-alls had shown up for this makeshift coven.

"Why do you have him tied up?" Thena asked, taking a step toward the women, but looking past them at Randy who looked angrier than a mad dog.

Her heart raced in her chest, her palms so damp that she rubbed them against her jeans while she fought to keep her nerves at bay. There was very little magic, other than their belief in her mother, and in her. The evil coming from the man bound in the chair all but consumed that faith. She sensed something similar to what she'd seen in Nate and Tommy Joe. She swallowed a lump that had formed in her throat. She didn't fear evil, but she damn sure wished she understood it.

"He was destroying my house, Thena. And that's not my Randy. He's a good boy, hard-working. Something bad is in him and you can get it out. Please take it out of my boy." Maxine's pleading tugged at Thena's heart.

She looked at the older woman, knowing Maxine believed she had some gift—a gift that Thena barely understood, and hadn't noticed until earlier today. She wasn't at all sure she could calm the evil inside Randy.

Have faith in what you can do. Priapus' words rang through her mind.

The other women in the room murmured their consolations to Maxine, and at the same time encouraged Thena to step forward.

"Show us your power," several of them said. "Show us how you can destroy the devil."

Thena glanced over at her mother, who watched her intently. She'd walked out on her mother earlier today, but at the moment, she saw no hostility in her mother's gaze. Her expression was full of concern. Thena was being put on the spot, powers she wasn't sure about herself being demanded from her. Yet her mother had told her just several hours ago that she was the daughter of a god. And she knew what Priapus was capable of. If she had just half his powers, surely she could make the demon leave this man.

"Randy? Do you want that evil pulled out of you?" she asked, moving between two of the women.

The handle of one of the brooms brushed up against her foot. A wall of evil was confined behind those broomsticks. It was like a balloon of thick humidity, nasty and foul-smelling, that surrounded the man in the chair.

Randy jerked against his ties, howling something incoherent, muffled by the bandana that was tied around his face, covering his mouth. She wondered how these women had managed to tie him down with the aggression he displayed at the moment.

His arms and legs were bound to the chair with clothesline. The women shifted uneasily around the edge of their circle, watching her and Randy. She sensed their excitement, their fear, and their trust. Every one of them believed she could cure Randy of whatever afflicted him.

No pressure there. Shit.

More than anything she wanted her herbs, her spell book. She wanted to be able to analyze the situation, figure out the best approach in confronting evil. She wanted to meditate, take the matter slowly, and study different spells until she was comfortable with the right one for this setting. But she hadn't been given that opportunity with little Nate. Then she'd just reacted, without any premeditation.

Thena took a step into the circle. The sensation to hold her breath, while pushing into the denseness of the evil overwhelmed her.

"Don't enter the circle, Thena," her mother warned. "His evil is very strong and we've confined it within the magic of the circle."

"The demon can't touch me, Mom. He isn't strong enough." Her words had Randy fighting furiously with the clothesline that held him to his chair.

She wasn't at all sure that was the case. But the calmness of her tone seemed to relax the energy in the women around her, making them stronger. Building their confidence in her enabled them to build a stronger wall against the evil. They didn't realize it, well, maybe her mother did, but they would aid her in fighting this monster that lurked inside Randy.

The women around her murmured under their breath, voicing their belief that she would be able to destroy the demon. They knew what she had done with little Nate.

She sucked in a breath, needing their strength to build her own. This had worked once before, and all she could do was pray it would work again.

Priapus had told her he would be there if she needed him. More than belief that she could wipe out this demon, she believed in Priapus.

"You aren't that strong, are you?" She stared deep into Randy's black eyes. His face contorted while he chewed at the cloth stuffed in his mouth.

She noticed blood mix with sweat where the clothesline rubbed against his wrists. There wasn't much time. The creature inside Randy would hurt him before she could save him if she weren't careful.

"In fact, you can't overtake a bunch of old women." Her words had Randy jumping off the ground, pulling the chair off of its legs until it toppled, with him still bound to it, onto its side on the floor. "Randy is sick of you being inside him," she continued, ignoring the cries of the women around her.

Tension built in the room. The candles danced, their flames casting shadows up the walls and throughout the room. Thena didn't dare take her gaze away from Randy, the thought that the evil inside him might leap out and into another one of the women bothering her. Somehow she would have to destroy it once it left Randy's body.

Thena licked her suddenly too dry lips, the room and its contents seeming to fade around her, as did all the women. All of her concentration was on Randy.

The urge to cite some incantation wouldn't leave her. If she could think of some fancy words, some prose that would rattle even the dead, terrify the shit out of the evil inside the man on the floor in front of her, it would at least give her something to do. She didn't make a habit of fighting evil though, and for the life of her she couldn't think of a damn word at the moment that even remotely sounded strong and unyielding. Not to mention her mouth was dryer than sandpaper.

Always her magic had been conjured up as the result of actions. Now she would have to rely simply on her will, on thinking it would happen, and believing that it would.

Randy's eyes looked like they would bulge out of his head as he struggled to look up at her. She took another step forward until she was less than a foot away from his body writhing on the floor. His body contorted, making the chair scrape against the hard wood floor.

His knee hit her foot and an icy cold rushed through her. She narrowed her gaze on him, remaining focused on his eyes—the windows to his soul. All of the evil inside him seemed to rush through her, like an electrical jolt, filling every inch of her body.

She wasn't sure, but it seemed like at least one of the women behind her screamed, although she didn't know why. Something inside her seemed to explode, filling her until she was sure she couldn't take anymore.

The evil was there, yet there was something else. It was part of her, as if something inside her had awoken for the first time. Strength—power—a rush that made her feel high and dizzy all at the same time.

"You are no match for me," she heard herself say. "Evil, you are dead."

Randy stood up so quickly that for a moment she thought he was no longer bound to the chair. Whatever possessed him was so strong that it enabled him to jump up, still confined to the chair, and stand awkwardly on his feet. He reminded her of a turtle, trying to stand with its house on its back. His body stiffened, his eyes large and filled with fear.

"You heard me," she whispered, her voice sounding strange even to her. It was too deep, off-pitch. "The evil is dead within you, Randy. You will be fine now."

She no more got the words out of him than he collapsed, his body and chair making a loud thump against the floor. Something seemed to fly out of him, something dark and gruesome.

It was the evil, and it wasn't dead. It was trying to escape.

Now what the fuck was she supposed to do!

The twisted entity seemed to hover above all of them, its misshapen mouth opening in a sneering grin, if that is what it could be called. Thena saw no lips, just a hollow opening in a face so gaunt and distorted she could barely stand to look at it.

"You are no match for me, witch," it howled with a voice so shrill it gave her chills.

"I am no witch," she cried out, speaking before she could give her words thought.

At the same time she jumped into the air, leaving the ground as she lunged at the gruesome creature. "I cast you to hell, you shall harm no more. I cast you to hell, you shall harm no more. I cast you to hell, you shall harm no more!"

She spoke so quickly, the words flowing out of her with a mind of their own. The creature screamed, dissipating into thin air leaving nothing but dust to filter slowly to the ground.

Thena didn't fall slowly. More like she crashed, suddenly feeling so weak she couldn't stop herself. The strength of Priapus seemed to wrap around her as she faded into blackness.

"Did you hear what she said?" Maxine Poller was the first to break into the circle.

"Her words didn't mean a thing." Margaret rushed into the circle also, hurrying to her daughter's side.

"She said she wasn't a witch." One of the ladies who'd been invited over to help build the strength of a coven stood planted to the ground.

None of the other women dared enter the area marked off by the brooms. Most of them trembled in their shoes, although none of them would admit it.

Priapus remained standing over Thena, knowing her newfound strength had drained her human body. She lay asleep at his feet, and it was all he could do to let her mother approach and kneel next to her daughter. He watched Triton walk through the wall, his attention riveted on the two women at his feet.

None of the women saw the two gods. Not even Margaret had the strength to sense their presence. But Priapus couldn't stay away from Thena any longer. He glared at the man who was her birth father, who'd given Thena half of who she was. No matter—he wasn't going to budge from where he stood protecting her.

"Not yet, my friend," Priapus warned him.

Triton looked up at him, his powers an equal match to Priapus', although his hesitation giving Priapus the advantage.

"You have no right to her." Priapus would be damned if this man would console Thena without her knowing about it.

Triton crossed his arms over his thick-barreled chest. "You heard her admit to her heritage. All the humans here heard her."

Margaret looked around at the group of ladies, oblivious to the arguing gods right next to her. "What happened in this room stays in this room, you all agreed to it."

Maxine worked to untie her son from the chair. He was limp and drenched in sweat, but didn't fight her. The demon was gone.

"She saved my boy," Maxine said to Margaret. "I owe her our lives for that."

"Then you keep your mouth shut about what happened here," Margaret hissed at her. "My daughter don't need no trouble. And you know as well as me if word gets out, there will be no peace for her."

The two women exchanged silent stares, an unspoken communication as the two mothers hovered over their beloved children.

"I want to know what she is, if she isn't a witch." A thin white woman pursed her lips and crossed her arms over her flat chest. "Margaret Cooke, I've known you all my life. You have never done anything like what that child of yours just did. How did she do that?"

"Yes. How did she fly up in the air like that?" Several other of the women questioned what they had just seen.

"And you saw her. Every bit of her glowed when she leapt into the air. I saw it with my own eyes."

Priapus didn't like this one bit. Thena's mother was right. There would be no rest among these humans once word got out about what Thena had done. He'd seen this same scene escalate out of control too many times over the centuries.

"Allow me," Triton said before Priapus could act. He waved his hand through the air, and then pointed to the front door. "As you each walk out that door, you shall forget what happened here today."

He nodded to Priapus. "It's the least I can offer my daughter."

With that he disappeared. And Priapus had to agree. After years of keeping his paternity a secret, it was the very least he could give her.

Chapter Thirteen

All order had left Thena's life. And she hated clutter—hated untidy situations. She always had.

She sat slumped on her couch, watching her mother and Gramma arrange the items on the coffee table.

"What is that?" Thena asked, staring at the towel that covered some object in her grandmother's arms.

"I haven't seen your looking-glass since I was a child." Margaret slid a chair so that it faced Thena on the other side of the coffee table.

"No reason to use it unless it's important." Gramma accepted the chair, placing the towel-covered object on to the table in front of her. "Thena, the glass ball will tell us what we need to know."

Margaret hurried out of the room, clamoring in the kitchen briefly before returning. "I've started water to boil. Tea will be ready when you are done."

Her Gramma nodded, her expression solemn while she fixed her gaze on Thena.

That glass ball probably wouldn't tell her where Priapus was right now. He'd been at Maxine Poller's house, she'd been sure of it. Somehow he managed to keep her from seeing him, or any of the women from seeing him. His smell had been wrapped around her, his fingers had brushed over her skin. But then when her mother had hurried her out of there, telling the women they had much work to do, she'd lost him. It drove her nuts that he appeared and then disappeared out of her life so easily. And it made her even crazier that where he might be right now distracted her thoughts so much.

"It's time." Gramma stared at Thena, wrinkles accentuated around her mouth when she pursed her lips. "There is a lot of work to do here. We need to focus and create a plan."

"Whenever you're ready." Margaret pulled up another chair, so that the three of them formed a triangle around the object on the coffee table.

Gramma pulled the towel away, and then unwrapped a convex-shaped glass from silky material that had been underneath the towel. She caressed the glass with her old hands, closing her eyes. Thena had never seen her grandmother do anything like this, and for a moment her actions reminded Thena of the fortune-tellers seen on TV.

The rounded glass had its underside painted black, and rested in a triangular-shaped frame. Gramma moved it so that each corner of the frame pointed at the three women. She continued caressing the glass.

"Prepare the water," she said, and Margaret stood, hurrying out of the room.

"What should I do?" Thena didn't like feeling awkward during an incantation. Somehow the spells didn't always work right unless everyone was comfortable with their task.

Her mother and Gramma weren't enlightening her, although it wasn't the first time. Many of her spells had been learned simply by watching. Her Gramma didn't answer. Thena pressed her lips together, knowing more questions would be futile.

"Grab the pouch of dragon's blood," her mother told her, returning to the room holding a steaming bowl of water.

The gentle smell of chamomile filled the air around her. "It doesn't need too much," Gramma said from her chair.

Thena sifted her fingers through the small rocks, which were actually dried sap commonly called dragon's blood. She dropped a palmful into the steaming water.

"Let Thena bless the glass." Gramma took her hands from the glass and leaned over for her bag. She pulled out a folded white cloth. Giving it a shake, Thena realized it was actually a small dress. "Your baptism gown," Gramma explained. "I still remember the day we took you down to the pond so the Goddess could make you part of the community. Soak it in the hot water and then rub it over the glass. You will clear the way so that we can see what we need to see."

The water was almost too hot to put her hand into but Thena did as she was instructed, wringing the small dress out carefully before kneeling next to the glass and wiping it clean. She stared into the convex shape, the dark glass gleaming once it was wet. The evil that had filled the Poller home, and her triumphant realization that she was stronger, took over her thoughts while she held the small dress. Wiping it slowly around the glass, she wondered at the evil's source.

Tell me where the evil comes from. Her thoughts jumped to Priapus. He never seemed to be too far out of her mind since she'd met him. And then, unwillingly, she thought about Triton, the sea god. Wouldn't both of them have the strength to clean these creatures out of Barren?

"We call to the spirits to show us the truth," Gramma began.

Thena leaned back, sitting on the couch and watching her grandmother and mother.

She repeated herself and then Margaret joined in.

"We call to the spirits to show us the truth."

The two women continued to repeat themselves and Thena felt their strength grow around her. She joined in the chant.

"We call to the spirits to show us the truth."

The three of them sat around the glass orb, their chant fading to whispers while Gramma caressed the smooth damp surface of the glass.

"By the power of three, we were meant to be. Maiden, witch and old crow are we." Gramma's words would have been funny. The solemn expression on her face eliminated the humor though. And her old magic swarmed around her, warming the room. "Committed to help. Burdened with strength, we follow your guidance. So mote it be."

Gramma's hands rose from the glass, her arms still extended as she stared into the glass orb. Her words faded and her body straightened. Thena watched her, fascinated. Gramma appeared to have gone into some kind of trancelike state, her expression changing as if she saw something in her mind.

"You must share the truth," Margaret encouraged. "Tell us what you see."

Thena looked at her when her mother reached under the coffee table, pulling out the old handheld tape recorder that Thena had used as a child to record her favorite songs from the radio. Her mother placed it on the coffee table, pushing two buttons to make it start recording. Thena looked from the recorder to her Gramma who had started mumbling gibberish.

Gramma finally said something that grabbed Thena's attention. "No one can tell what happened."

Thena opened her mouth to ask what that meant, but her mother raised her hand to silence her. Her gaze was intent on Gramma.

"She was nothing but a tramp anyway. You know she enjoyed it. Things just got out of hand. No use anyone getting in trouble over a no-good like her anyway." Gramma didn't sound like herself, her expression changing as she spoke.

Thena watched her, trying to figure out what the hell she was talking about. Her grandmother's expression had hardened. She looked defiant. Her eyes opened suddenly looking straight at Thena. Her gaze was glassy though, as if she saw something else that wasn't in the room.

"She was a damn good fuck though." Gramma started laughing.

Margaret's hand went to her mouth, but Thena kept her attention on Gramma. Never had she ever heard the old woman use profanity of any kind.

"No matter that she's dead. We just ain't gonna let no one know the truth. The likes of her would end up with kid, and her kind ain't meant to be mothering."

Gramma almost sounded like a man. Chills rushed over Thena. Her Gramma was repeating a conversation that had taken place at another time. Something terrible and disgusting had happened. More than anything she wanted to encourage her Gramma to share what she saw, who she was repeating. Her heart raced as she watched the sneer fade from her Gramma's face. A tear started down her wrinkled cheek. Sadness filled the air around them. Thena watched in amazement.

"It hurts. I hate you all. You're gonna pay for this." Gramma's voice cracked, and her body sagged in the chair.

She looked down at her lap, and for a moment, it looked like she'd left her trance. But then she murmured, her voice so quiet that Margaret lifted the recorder and held it close to Gramma, so it could pick up what she said.

"I never said you all could do this. You raped me. I told you no. All of you will rot for this. I hate you. Everyone of you. And none of you care squat for me, you never did. It hurts. I can't make it quit hurting. It hurts so damned bad."

Thena stared into the dark glass. It glowed on the coffee table, letting off an eerie light that captivated her attention. Images moved. She saw them and held her breath, desperately trying to bring things into focus. The fabric of the couch prickled against the back of her legs and she scooted forward, intent on what she saw.

There were people, and they moved quickly, jumping in and out of focus as if they pounced on something and ran into each other. And then she heard the cries, painful, gut-wrenching cries. The more the images moved, the louder the wailing sounded.

Thena wanted to cover her ears, close her eyes, jump up and run from the grotesque sight that barely focused in front of her. She saw men, a handful of men, and a naked woman, crying, screaming, begging them to stop raping her. The more she screamed, the faster the men moved. Nothing would stop them. The urge to do something made her gut twist in hard knots. Jump into the scene, grab the images that blurred in front of her, anything to stop this horrendous crime from happening.

But it had already happened. That much she seemed to know. Thena wasn't seeing the future, but the past. A nasty crime had embedded their community with hatred and evil.

Gramma started crying like a baby, rocking back and forth until she slumped forward. Margaret set down the recorder quickly and jumped up to grab her mother before she fell out of the chair.

"Someone brought this evil to Barren," she said to Thena.

Thena stared wide-eyed at her mother who held her grandmother in her arms. Sadness and pain surrounded her with so much intensity that she couldn't shake it. She had no idea who the woman was, or who the men were, but a terrible crime had been committed. What terrified her was that she somehow knew they had gotten away with it.

Slowly she stood, realizing her Gramma was done, and very drained from the experience. "Let's put her on the couch," she suggested, coming around to help lift the old woman and make her comfortable.

"I've only seen her enter a trance once before and it drained her then." Margaret covered the glass with the silk cloth that had been around it originally and then hurried into the kitchen, returning with a damp washcloth. "I worried she was too old to do this again."

Gramma's eyes fluttered open, the brightness in them having returned. "Who are you calling old, child?" she reprimanded, soothing the mood of the room instantly.

Thena reached out to pause the recorder, letting her mother and Gramma scold each other while she went into the kitchen to make fresh tea.

A terrible crime had taken place here. She didn't know when, or by whom, but something told her that finding out was imperative if she were to set things right.

The cassette was playing back when she returned to the living room, her Gramma watching wide-eyed, obviously hearing for the first time what she'd said while in her trance.

"This town was cursed," Gramma informed them. "They murdered some poor gal and she cursed the lot of us."

"I wonder who she was," her mother said, and then glanced at Thena. "I didn't know this when we sought you out. You had to come home. Your Gramma and I knew you had to be here. But now I know why. It was more than sharing the truth of your birth with you. The three of us have a lot of work to do here."

Thena didn't say anything until she had tea ready. She prepared sandwiches too. Her Gramma needed protein after the strength of the spell had worn off. Performing magic at that level always depleted the body. Thena prepared the table and then helped her Gramma into the kitchen where they sat and ate.

"I saw it happen in the glass," she announced after a few moments of silence.

Her mother and grandmother stopped eating, both of them looking up at her.

"You saw the violence." Gramma nodded, her glassy, dark eyes moist as if she wished Thena hadn't seen.

"What did you see?" Margaret looked at both of them, putting her sandwich on her plate.

Thena had lost her appetite too. "There were four…maybe five men." The images she'd seen in the glass resurfaced, plaguing her emotions as she talked about it. "And a woman screaming, begging them to stop."

Her heart suddenly seemed too heavy for her chest. She glanced from her mother to her grandmother, the silence in the kitchen weighted down with sadness.

"Are we sure this happened here in Barren?" Margaret asked. "I've never heard of such a crime."

"Too often crimes like this are never reported to the authorities." Thena shook her head, willing the ugly scene to leave her head. "And in this case it wasn't just rape, but murder."

"We will go out tonight and search the souls at the cemetery," Gramma decided and then reached for her sandwich.

Thena knew she could get faster answers if she talked to Priapus. She believed now that he was truly a god, capable of so much more than she was. It dawned on her that possibly he held back, allowing her to come to terms with her own powers. He'd told her it would take time to come to terms with being a goddess—that her work was cut out for her.

That thought in itself unnerved her. It would be opening a can of worms if she asked Priapus to share everything he knew. She didn't believe she was meant to know everything. Not to mention, messing with powers that she didn't understand would render her out of control. And Thena didn't like not being in control.

She would gather her answers on her own. But she would do more than wander a cemetery.

Chapter Fourteen

Thena almost shrieked when she reached to open her mother's car door and it was opened for her. Priapus stood to the side so she could get out.

"What are you doing here?" she asked, trying to regain her wits about her.

It bothered her that she'd been so lost in thought she hadn't sensed his strength until he'd been right next to her.

"I was about to ask you the same." Priapus took her arm, moving her so he could shut her car door.

He turned so they faced each other, his brooding expression making her feel he could search through her thoughts to gather any information he wished. She hated that, and did her best to clamp down on any thoughts in her head, any emotions, and meet his stare. Such concentration made it really hard to comment though, so she simply stared up at him.

The slightest twitch of his mouth gave her cause to believe he sensed what she was doing, and thinking. Damn.

"You don't know what you're getting yourself into," he told her, pulling slightly on her arm, willing her to move so that they touched.

Thena fought for calm, offering him a smug smile. "You don't know what I'm doing at all. Therefore, you don't know what I'm getting into either."

She prayed she was right, hoping with everything she had that he wouldn't sense she was searching out the source of evil in the town. Doing this on her own would help her come to terms with her powers. She just knew that in her heart to be true.

Priapus' look hardened.

He didn't like the way she'd successfully pulled her thoughts from him. And he liked it even less that she openly admitted to it, and challenged him at the same time.

"I will not allow you to walk into trouble." He would damn well see to it that she didn't.

No matter that she succeeded in keeping her thoughts from him. It was obvious by her expression that she was up to something she knew he wouldn't approve of. Determination showed in the way she pursed her lips. She stood tall, daring anyone to challenge her. Knowing she'd taken on challenges most of her life, and more than likely often won, had its appeal. He gazed down at her soft features, still so feminine in spite of her willful expression.

A gentle breeze had picked up since morning, countering the heat of the midday sun, and lifting Priapus' hair around his head. She decided she liked this latest look he sported, casual and carefree, with an expression that let anyone know he wasn't a man to be messed with.

"I'm a big girl," she said, adding a teasing tone to her voice. She batted her eyes at him purposefully. "I can take care of myself."

"You are a lady, my dear, not a girl. And I will see to your protection." He cupped her chin, lifting her face so he could brush his lips over hers.

Although the town was quiet during this part of the day, more than one inquisitive soul would see her kissing a man they'd never laid eyes on before. She had a feeling that Priapus knew this, and didn't give a damn that he was making a silent statement to the community. Granted she was thirty years old, and had been away from Barren for years, but this was a small town, word traveled. If she'd come back home with a man by her side that would be one thing. But she hadn't. And no one in town knew Priapus. He didn't seem to care that she was openly showing affection to a man that no one in town knew.

The community would just have to get over it. At the moment, all she wanted was to be in his arms.

Mine. The thought that he would make such a public claim on her sent a rush of chills over her skin. She went up on tiptoe, deepening the kiss before she gave too much thought to the consequences.

Over the past day or so, spending all of her time with Gramma and her mother, she'd missed this cocky man. His arrogance, his self-confidence, and those damn sexy good looks of his, hadn't left her thoughts the entire time she'd been away from him. He was becoming more than an infatuation.

But there was work to do. She broke off the kiss with a sigh. "Isn't there something you should be doing?" she asked before she bothered to open her eyes.

"I'm doing it," he breathed into her face.

Thena chuckled, although his words sent a hot flush over her skin. It had been several days since they'd fucked, and with a mere kiss he had her body in an uproar, her pussy throbbing while her nipples hardened with an ache that she knew he could appease.

She slipped around him, moving toward the front of her car and the sidewalk of the quiet downtown area.

"Then you need to find something else to do," she said quickly over her shoulder. "I have errands."

Priapus knew she was up to something. She headed toward a hardware store, but he doubted she was shopping for supplies to do home improvement. The shop was full of demons, and she was walking into their lair. He didn't like this—things could get ugly. They would see her for what she was, before she realized who they were. He crossed his arms, watching her tight ass sway away from him, and wrapped his protection around her.

There was no way she could look back, and she didn't have to. Priapus' powers swam around her protectively, and she had to admit she liked the feeling of knowing he was so close at hand.

She would do this without his help though. She had to. The only way a witch came to terms with her powers was to walk the path alone, feel her strength, not allow it to mingle with others. She had no clue what a goddess might do, but knew in her heart that this was what she had to do.

The bell on the door rang cheerfully when she pushed it open and entered the store. Shelves of nuts and bolts greeted her and she glanced briefly at the posterboard sign, *Willey's Hardware, everything you need with one stop*.

Thena could only wish everything she needed would be here with one stop.

"Hi, Randy," she said cheerfully, when she spotted Randy Poller behind the counter.

"Well, Thena Cooke!" Randy's face lit up with a sincere smile. "When did you get back in town?"

She searched his face, seeing the sincerity of his greeting. Randy didn't remember her being at his house the other day. Well, this would be interesting.

He also showed no signs of hostility, or anger, or hatred. The evil she'd cast out of him was gone, but apparently so were his memories of it. Oddly though, there was a cold evil lingering in the store. Its coldness hit her hard, making the otherwise cheerful-looking shop seem dangerous. Trepidation seeped through her.

"I've been home for several days now." She decided it was best not to question why he didn't remember.

Sunshine streamed through the large bay windows at the front of the store. Dust bunnies floated through the air, giving the area a relaxed appearance. The look was deceiving though. Hostility sat heavy in the air. One or two customers lingered in the long aisles, and several men chatted at the counter. Thena was the only woman in the store. She smiled at Randy but kept her guard up, trying to locate the source of the evil that chilled the place.

"You running this place now?" She noticed the men standing around the counter turned and watched her warily.

Randy frowned as if trying to remember something. "No. I just work here. Is there something I can help you find?"

She was focusing more on trying to read the feelings of the others in the store and his question took her off-guard. With a quick gesture of her hand, she tried to make a show of not remembering the name of the item she needed.

"Mom has a drip in her bathroom sink that is driving me nuts. I thought I'd try and fix it for her."

Randy nodded and led the way down one of the aisles, putting her within a few feet of the men at the counter. Hostility swarmed around the lot of them. Turning her attention to the small group, she tried to recognize them. For the most part they were older, out of her peer group. Their faces were vaguely familiar but none of them were men she had known when she lived here before. Thena guessed that each of them possessed one of those demons in them that she'd cast out of Randy.

He didn't seem to notice their hostility. "More than likely you'll need to take off the cover on the faucet handle and replace the insides to stop that leak. It's not too hard to do."

Randy held up a see-through plastic faucet handle, trying to show her what needed to be done.

"Seems the like of her would just cast a spell on it," one of the men at the counter mumbled.

Thena turned her attention toward them to see the three men hovering around the counter scowl at her.

"Do you think that would work?" She wouldn't let them intimidate her. "Maybe I should just cast a spell on one of you so that you'll come out and fix it for me."

They all straightened, realizing she wouldn't cower, yet noticeably upset by her comment.

"I have the right to refuse service to anyone." The man behind the counter sucked in his thick belly, his black eyes glowing with fury.

Thena smiled. Their blatant outrage over her comment had let down all of their guards. Emotions surged toward her. They hated her, despised her, and that didn't surprise her in the least. But there was more. Fear, worry, concern that she could hurt them. Those were the emotions she focused on.

Her heart raced but she would do this. Randy looked rather hesitant as he held the pieces she needed for her mother's sink in his hand. She nodded for him to put the items on the counter and stepped forward so that she stood between the two men leaning on her side of the register.

"This is all I need," she said, taking her time to look at each man next to her.

The man to her left balled his fists, creases increasing in his forehead as he glared at her. There was no justifying this amount of anger. All she'd done was come in here to make a simple purchase. But if each of them had the same evil in them that Randy had been possessed with, that would explain their animosity.

That knowledge didn't ease her tension.

"I'm not selling you shit." The man behind the counter waved a hand at Randy. "Put it back on the shelves." And then he turned a hateful eye at Thena. "And you need to get out of here. We don't want your kind around here."

Anyone overhearing his words might have thought the man a bigot. But Thena understood his meaning. His animosity had nothing to do with the color of her skin. The demon inside the man spoke, hating her for the powers she had.

Well, his hatred could only mean they feared her. Doing her best not to start shaking, even though her heart raced way too fast in her chest, she inhaled slowly, daring to meet his gaze.

"You are the ones who need to leave," she hissed, hoping and praying she stifled her fear, and the creatures inside these men didn't sense it. "The men you possess are tired of you being inside them."

Her breath caught in her throat when the men on either side of her, and the man behind the counter started laughing.

"She's an absolute nut," the man next to her hooted.

Sweat trickled between her breasts, although it wasn't warm in the hardware store. The front door chimed, and she felt the power of Priapus surround her before she looked his way. His green eyes were dark with emotion as he sauntered easily toward her and the men. The confidence emanating around him would have anyone thinking he had known the lot of them all of his life.

His look turned hostile when he reached her side. "You're dead. All of you!" he hissed, placing one hand on her shoulder while waving his other hand at the men.

His controlled strength was so raw, so carnal, Thena's pussy swelled with a primal ache before she could control her reaction to him.

The man behind the counter fell backwards, losing his footing and rattling everything on the shelves behind him. The men on either side of her stiffened, then started coughing, as if someone had been choking them and now they gasped for breath.

Priapus had stood back as long as he dared. He'd give Thena credit for being willing to walk into a nest of demons, but she didn't have a clue how to call forth her powers to get rid of them. Her confidence in her strength still didn't exist.

He glanced over at Randy. "Sell the lady the parts she needs," he said quietly.

Randy hurried around the counter, giving the other man a worried look before stepping in front of him to work the register.

Priapus curved his finger around Thena's shoulder and then caressed her arm. He'd frustrated her, but he sensed her fear ebb. The damn woman just wanted to take on too much, too quickly. Her stubbornness to try and do everything on her own would get her seriously hurt, and he realized she didn't see that.

It was time again to give her a serious eye-opener.

Waiting until she'd accepted the small bag and paid for the items, he then slid his hand down her back. "We have other errands to run. Shall we go?"

Thena glared at him, but then turned a curious look to the men at the counter.

"Are you okay?" she asked the man who refused her sale at the register.

The older guy laughed, an embarrassed sound, and ran thick fingers over his forehead, wiping his hair back. "Just fine, miss. Not sure what came over me. You have a good day, you hear?"

Randy looked beyond baffled.

Thena wondered if any of them remembered anything that had just happened, or if they had known all along the demons had been in them and were now just trying to cover up for the terrible behavior they'd displayed while possessed by the creatures.

"I'll have a good day." She shrugged free of Priapus, and smiled reassuringly at all of the men. "If any of you need anything, you let me know."

The men turned to her, smiles fading. A sadness almost appeared on their expressions. They had been aware of their atrocious behavior. She realized that at that moment. Their pride and confusion toward the matter wouldn't allow them to discuss it with her, but she could see it plain as day on their faces.

Nothing else was said, and she turned, knowing Priapus waited, more than likely so he could lecture her for not letting him handle the matter in the first place. Well, he could lecture all he wanted. She'd been doing fine. Just because she'd been a little scared, didn't mean she couldn't handle getting rid of those nasty creatures.

"You've got all the answers, do you?" Priapus whispered when they'd left the store.

"I doubt anyone has all of the answers." She turned on him, putting her hands on her hips. "Even a god," she added under her breath.

It was all Priapus could do not to lift her off the ground and give her a sound shaking. She was more intelligent than this. Her stubbornness was blinding her, making her say things he doubted she really believed.

He moved into her, not taking his gaze from those beautiful brown eyes while he backed her into the car parked in the street next to them.

"Maybe I should remind you exactly what a god is capable of," he whispered, pressing her arms against her sides.

Her breasts pushed together, accentuating some very nice cleavage. "What are you doing? People will see us."

Letting go of her arms, he gripped her breasts, enjoying how her nipples hardened instantly against his palms. His long shaft grew instantly and he leaned into her, letting her see how damned horny she made him.

"Priapus!" she hissed, unable to stop the way he turned her on. A flush of embarrassment rushed through her though. "You can't do this in the middle of downtown."

"Do you not have faith in the gods you seek guidance from?" he asked, taking his gaze from her momentarily to look over her head at the quiet downtown area. "No one can see us now. They don't know we're standing here, getting ready to fuck."

She gasped, her heart skipping a beat while her breath suddenly came in pants. "We aren't going to fuck in the middle of downtown," she managed to whisper, shocked he would suggest such a thing.

"Oh, yes we are." He ran his hands down her front and gripped her hips, thrusting his cock hard against her. "And you should be ashamed of your lack of belief. You pray to your gods yet you have no faith in their abilities?"

The way he touched her, pushed against her, made it hard to think straight. His hard body with corded muscles aligned with hers, allowing her to feel his strength, his solid and slow heartbeat, his raw power as it penetrated through her.

"I don't need you to mock me." It was all she could do to think straight with him so close.

Priapus ran his hands under her skirt at the same time that two teenagers sauntered down the sidewalk chatting to each other. His hand moved between her legs, cupping her heat. The distraction of the kids almost unnerved her. She trembled, unable to look away from them. But they didn't look toward her or Priapus, just kept on walking.

Priapus slid a finger into her moist folds, brushing against her clit. She gripped his shoulders, his touch sending ripples of lust rushing through her.

"You are a wicked man," she gasped, clinging to him while he encouraged her orgasm.

"Hardly, my dear," he whispered, enjoying how her cheeks flushed when she was ready to come.

She ran her hands down his chest, feeling his muscles mold and flex against her palms. It was necessary to learn every inch of him. And although she knew fucking him in the street, or in a field on a magical bed, didn't allow her all the time she needed to know this man, it was imperative that she put as much of him to memory as she could.

The reasons why didn't seem to matter. She just *knew*. The realization of that made her heart swell, begin beating at a slightly different pace. Placing her palm against his heart she reveled in the fact that his heartbeat matched hers. They were meant to be together—soul mates.

At that moment, Priapus thrust inside her pussy with his fingers, pushing her over the edge. She collapsed against him, keeping her hand against his heart, feeling their pulses soar together.

"Together we are one," she conceded, although she meant to say it to herself, and was almost sure that she had.

"It's about time you saw the truth." Priapus slid his fingers out of her, leaving her damp and needing more.

She hadn't meant to speak out loud. And he knew the revelation of their uniting had just hit her. Undoing his pants, he watched her brown eyes swirl with the knowledge, deep dark pools of wisdom, yet swimming with curiosity over what she still hadn't come to terms with.

Damn it to hell, she was fucking beautiful. And she was his. He'd sensed the knowledge just moments before she had. There was one perfect soul mate for every being. Some searched a lifetime for their partner. Few were lucky enough to stumble on them at an early age. And many never mated with their true match. Priapus could hardly contain himself from the happiness that soared through him that they'd met, and now were together. Thena was meant to be his—and he was meant to be hers.

His cock jumped free of confinement, dancing with need once he'd slid it out of his jeans. Such confining clothes. Humans had done better in past centuries with their fashions.

Thena sucked in her breath, the throbbing between her legs intensifying when his giant cock sprang forth. An older woman passed behind Priapus on the street. He pushed away from Thena, allowing enough space between them that his too-large cock would have room.

Thena stifled a giggle when he gripped it with his hand, and turned his attention to the woman passing briefly. She didn't see them.

This was almost fun. "I see how easy it would be to escape from the worries of life with powers like this," she told him.

She wasn't sure why, but a cloud passed over his gaze, making his green eyes darken at her words.

"Come here," he said, instead of commenting on what she'd just said. "Let me show you something."

He wouldn't admit it to her, but Thena had just struck a nerve. For so many centuries he'd run from any commitment. Humans had disowned him, mocked him, made him feel unwanted. He'd left Earth, allowing his powers to fulfill him, entertain him, and keep him free of any responsibility. What Thena just said was true. It could almost be fun to ignore the world, live in his own fantasies, and forget about everyone else's problems. But that sort of life hadn't fulfilled him, and he knew it wouldn't fulfill Thena either.

For this moment, they would enjoy their privacy, protected by his powers. But in the end, he guessed their true happiness would come from growing stronger together, and helping others. The way it had been meant to be for all eternity.

He ran his hands against her hips and then down her inner thigh, lifting her leg. Thena held onto his shoulders, looking down when he positioned his cock between her legs.

Thick as her arm, and rock-hard, Priapus' cock reached for her pussy as if it had a mind of its own.

She draped her leg over his arm, standing on one foot while looking down between them. "You know damn well and good I'm not built to get you off, Priapus. This isn't fair to you."

And she wanted to satisfy him. But if he fucked her with that cock, it would do serious damage.

Their gazes met, and she knew he thought what she wondered. She wouldn't tear her gaze from his when his cock head pressed against her moist heat. The urge to close her eyes, focus on what she wanted to offer him, filled her and distracted her. But she wouldn't look away from him.

If she could adjust her body, allow herself to take Priapus' size, she would be able to offer him complete fulfillment. His smile told her he knew what she was about. She wasn't trying to hide her thoughts at the moment. It was too much wanting him, needing him, to worry about what he saw inside her. And truth be told, letting him see her feelings right now was a lot easier than telling him how desperately she needed him.

He thrust into her, holding her so she didn't lose her balance, and impaling her at the same time. She wanted to look down, to see that mighty cock glide inside her cunt. Just the thought of it made her come, explode against his shaft. Her muscles constricted, clinging to him while he moved deeper inside her.

"You were made for me," he whispered, leaning into her to nibble on her lip.

Her eyes fluttered, and she muttered something, but he captured it with his kiss. Never had a pussy felt so right, so perfect. She was like a glove made especially for him. He glided deep into her heat, standing on the street while the town continued about their business. Fucking her here, or anywhere, would be perfect. Thena was his. And that knowledge felt as good as his cock did sailing in and out of her hot cunt.

She dug into his shoulders with her fingers, feeling him impale her, that enormous cock take over her insides. Nothing she'd ever experienced or dreamed about came close to the way Priapus made her feel at that moment.

"Damn it. Priapus. Fuck yes." She no longer cared. He had to know how perfect he was. He certainly knew that he fulfilled her better than any man ever had, or could.

"That's it, baby, come for me, let me know how good this feels for you."

And it did feel so fucking good.

Her hands slid off his shoulders, feeling the strength in his biceps as his muscles bulged around her fingers.

Priapus cock split her in two, took over her entire being, and she loved every damn moment of it.

With her leg over his arm, she let her head fall back, allowing him even deeper into the heat of her passion.

That giant cock of his filled her. He was so damned big she swore he filled her clear through to her throat. The pressure would make her pass out. She damn well knew it. split her in two.

"Fuck me, Priapus," she cried out, accepting they were alone in the middle of downtown. Knowing and not caring that he had the powers to make anything happen that he wished.

"Oh yes, baby," he breathed, watching her breathe hard. Her nipples peaked against her dress, fueling his need for her.

He moved faster, enjoying how wet she was for him. Pounding her with his massive cock got her off, and the look on her face fed his need for her as much as the incredible feeling of her sweet muscles wrapped around his cock.

"You've got me, sweetheart, all of me," he told her, and exploded inside her.

Thena scraped her fingernails against his flesh, feeling him convulse inside her, shoot his cum so deep in her cunt. Her body embraced him, her muscles tightening with her own orgasm. Along with his cum, she felt some of his powers fill her too, and the revelation made her feel more alive, on fire with knowledge and serenity she never knew had existed before.

Chapter Fifteen

Maxine Poller rapped with determination on Margaret's back door. Thena had barely slipped out of her shoes after getting home, and hurried through the kitchen to see Maxine's face lighten through the window on the door when she saw her.

"Just who I wanted to see," she beamed when Thena opened the door. "It means so much to me what you did for my boy."

Thena raised an eyebrow, curious that Maxine remembered that Thena had cast out the demon, yet Randy didn't.

"Randy doesn't seem to remember that he was possessed." Thena took the still-warm loaves of bread that Maxine offered her.

Over the years she'd grown accustomed to receiving various gifts from people she'd been able to help with her magic, and had learned it often embarrassed and insulted people when she told them the gifts weren't necessary. Not to mention, any retirement money Margaret or her grandmother were bringing in couldn't possibly be enough to help feed Thena. She was appreciative.

"I thought you had something to do with that." Maxine returned to the doorway and lifted a large pot she must have put down when she knocked. "And here are some greens. I made them with ham hock. I remember how you loved them as a child."

"It all smells so good, and you're right, I love greens." Thena smiled, the rich scent of the greens tantalizing her nose.

Just moving to the counter, lifting the lid so she could sniff the wonderful food, was enough to let her feel the sore muscles that ached throughout her body. She was sore between her legs, yet at the same time throbbing as she craved him once again.

Priapus had been quick and thorough, fucking her in the street downtown. Sheez…just the thought made her feel like a tramp. Although she'd wanted it, and had thoroughly loved it. Okay, so a willing tramp. Good grief.

You are not a tramp, Priapus whispered in her ear, although when she turned her head she knew she was alone in the kitchen with Maxine.

Stay out of my thoughts. She knew he read her mind and scolded him for doing so, then quickly returned her attention to Maxine.

Maxine waved away Thena's thanks and then her expression turned contemplative. "It's been rather odd. Almost everyone at my house the other day has forgotten that they were there. Seemed to me that you and your mother didn't want a lot of talk, so made everyone forget."

Thena almost said she didn't have that kind of power. But she stopped herself. She knew someone who did have that kind of power. But why would Priapus make almost everyone forget that she'd cast the demon out of Randy, but not all of them?

"Maybe it was easier for some to cope with what happened by not remembering." She'd seen that happen before when intense magic took form.

Maxine seemed to accept the comment, and moved to the back door. "Well, I just wanted to thank you again," she said, reaching for the door handle.

"Maxine, may I ask you something?" Thena knew when the older woman's face lit up that she would share with Thena anything she knew.

"Why sure, honey. You ask me anything."

Thena arranged the loaves next to the crock pot on the counter. "Something terrible happened in Barren. I'm not sure when, and I don't think it was ever reported to the police. But I need to know what happened. I think a lady died because of it, because of some terrible crime, possibly rape."

She turned in time to see Maxine's face turn ashen.

"Where's your mama?" Maxine looked toward the doorways leading into the living room and then toward the stairs.

"I just got home. More than likely they're visiting." Which was what her mother and grandmother called it when they were called out into the town to help with this matter or that.

Worry lines creased her forehead before she turned toward the back door. "Don't be asking foolish questions, child."

Thena hurried toward her, taking Maxine's arm before she could open the back door. Maxine yanked her arm free and then turned, pointing a finger at Thena.

"Now I'm serious, girl. This is for your own good. Don't you go asking anyone questions like that. Whatever you think you might know, just forget about it."

And with that she opened the back door and hurried outside. Thena stared after her, stupefied, until she heard

Maxine's tires crack and pop over the driveway gravel when she backed out on to the road.

"Well, well," Priapus said from behind her.

And she turned, seeing him at the same time that his powers wrapped around her like a wonderful, favorite blanket. He reclined at the kitchen table, his long muscular legs stretched out. Her body temperature went up a few notches just looking at him.

"You really do need to learn to knock," she told him, although she was anything but upset at his sudden appearance.

Priapus cocked an eyebrow at her but didn't move. One elbow leaned on the table, an act that would get him thumped in the head if her Gramma saw it. And his legs stretched out with his ankles crossed, his straight-cut jeans and cowboy boots adding to his sinfully gorgeous appearance. The bulge in the crotch of his blue jeans was a reminder of what he had, and the tingling that rushed through her at the sight of him was enough to remind of her of how he had so recently made her feel.

Her mouth went dry, and then just as quickly was almost too moist for her to speak. "You know about the crime that took place here." It wasn't a question.

"So now you suddenly want my help?" His hooded gaze made it hard to read if he mocked her or not.

She crossed her arms, wishing she could figure him out. "I want to set this town straight."

Priapus nodded once but said nothing. Instead he turned his attention to the doorway that led to the dining room. At the same time the front door opened.

Gramma appeared in the doorway a moment later, with Margaret behind her. The two of them looked from her to Priapus, who continued to lounge at the kitchen table.

"Sit up straight, boy." Gramma kicked him in the foot when she entered the room and placed her purse on the counter. "I see Maxine Poller has brought her payment."

Thena wasn't surprised by her grandmother's callous reaction to Priapus' presence in her daughter's home. Margaret, on the other hand, remained in the doorway, staring at him, and then slowly turned her attention to her daughter.

"I don't believe we've met," she said politely, but the clarity in her tone gave indication she already didn't approve.

Thena sensed her mother's worry, and her grandmother's calm resolve. So like both of them with any new situation.

"Gramma, Mom, I'd like you to meet Priapus."

Priapus stood, filling the room, and stepped to the side so Gramma could sit. Margaret looked like she needed to sit down too, but remained in the doorway, taking in Priapus with a quick glance.

"If you're Priapus, then you've got a cock like a—" Gramma began.

Margaret gasped. "Mother!" she cried out, putting her hands on her hips and silencing the older woman who didn't look a bit remorseful about her candid comment.

"Well, he would." Gramma shot her daughter a reprimanding look and then looked at Thena. "Does he?"

Now Margaret did move to sit opposite her mother, suddenly looking very lost. "I feel the strength of his powers. We don't need to know any more details about his...anatomy."

"Where did you find her?" Gramma asked Priapus, her gaze wantonly traveling down him.

"I found her in Kansas City, the night she lost her job," Priapus answered, sounding very much like the young suitor trying to impress parents of a girl he wanted to date. "And then I followed her here."

"I sensed you in the airport." Margaret didn't look at him, but instead squinted at the window. "I thought you were Triton, keeping an eye on us."

"Triton didn't appear until you called him," Priapus said softly.

Margaret nodded, still not looking at any of them.

Thena saw that her mother very much loved Triton, and probably had kept him in her thoughts over the years. Hell, maybe she had snuck off for secret rendezvous. All the times that Thena had been alone growing up, thinking her mother was working, she might have been off seeing her dad. She didn't know what to think about that.

"So the chain continues," Gramma said, now turning her attention to Thena. "The daughter of a god now finds herself a god."

"Is that what this is?" Margaret didn't look too excited about the knowledge.

"If you're asking me if I'm going to find a man who will run out and leave me with child, the answer is no." Thena leaned into the counter, staring at her mother who met her gaze.

Margaret stiffened, her lips thinning into a pursed line. But Thena saw and sensed something else that didn't make sense to her.

Priapus surprised her by suddenly turning and reaching for the old teapot on the stove, and then moving to the sink to fill it with water. It was such an act of servitude that it didn't seem to fit him. She found herself watching him complete the simple task and so was distracted when her mother sighed, a sudden sadness wrapping around her that grabbed Thena's attention.

"Triton didn't leave me, Thena. I asked him to stay away."

"You did what?" Thena couldn't believe what she was hearing. "Why would you keep me from my father?"

Margaret looked down at her hands. Thena realized her mother had them fisted in her lap, and that she fought for serenity to explain decisions she had made so long ago. She gave Gramma a quick glance and then looked up at Thena. Her eyes were moist.

"At the time I thought it was best for you. You needed to learn how to be a witch before you could master being a goddess."

Priapus waved his hand over the counter and four good-sized mugs appeared. Any other time, Thena would be shocked at his display of powers. Under the circumstances, they somehow seemed fitting, as if he were silently adding to the conversation by showing how a god, or goddess, was so much more powerful than any witch would ever be.

"But I never even knew that you knew who my father was," Thena whined, realizing she sounded like a child, but unable to restrain the sudden wave of emotions that leapt forth. "How could you keep that from me?"

Margaret stood, approaching her daughter while a tear slowly drifted down her cheek. Thena realized her own eyes grew moist and she blinked furiously, willing her emotions not to get out of control. Slowly, her mother touched her arm, the gentle brushing of flesh comforting even though Thena wanted to be angry with her mother. She saw how the topic tore at her mother and didn't want her mother in pain.

"If I'd told you that I knew him then you would've wanted to meet him. He agreed with me shortly after you were born that he would allow you to grow up and develop naturally. I called for him when I knew it was time." Margaret accepted one of the mugs when Priapus handed it to her.

He offered the same brew to Gramma, and then finally gave a steaming cup to Thena.

"Drink," he ordered quietly.

Thena looked up at him, and he nodded silently to the cup. She blew at the hot drink before sipping, and then immediately felt the power of the tea when she swallowed. A soothing brew, created with simple, old-fashioned magic, so appropriate for the moment. Priapus had a compassionate side that continued to surprise her every time he showed it. He had realized the intense emotional scene about to play out, and helped everyone to remain calm with the specially prepared tea.

"I'm starting to think that you and Gramma know a lot more about these demons than you wanted me to think. You brought me here, knowing I had the power to call them out." Thena realized the tea helped her to think more clearly.

"We aren't strong enough to rid the town of the evil. And it was time." Gramma sounded as calm as she always did, as if she knew the future as clearly as she knew the past.

Usually that trait in her Gramma reassured Thena. But now it frustrated her. She took a larger sip of the sweet tea, and then put her mug on the counter.

"You two both know what crime took place here in this town. You know what spawned this evil. You couldn't stop it so you sent for me." Thena put her hands on her hips and glared at her mother and then her Gramma.

"Thena Lotus Cooke," Gramma hissed, using a tone that would have sent her running if Thena had still been a child. "How dare you accuse your mother and me of such a thing."

Margaret turned a harsh look at Priapus. "If you are indeed the god Priapus then why don't you eliminate the evil from our town?"

Priapus offered a gallant nod. "I'd be honored to help. So far, your daughter hasn't wanted my assistance."

"Kind of like her mother when it came to raising her precious daughter." Gramma spoke into her cup of tea.

Thena turned and looked at her Gramma, and then at her mother. She let out a loud sigh, the soothing effects of the tea making it hard to remain angry with the only family she had. Not to mention she loved the two women very much.

She put her hand on her mother's arm, capturing her mother's attention. "I'm glad you finally told me of my father. It will take time to get accustomed to the idea. But right now what confuses me is how you two don't know of this heinous crime when Maxine Poller obviously did."

Both Gramma and Margaret showed their immediate surprise.

"Maxine knew what happened to that poor girl?" Gramma asked, stunned.

Chapter Sixteen

She'd been here the other night with her Gramma and mother, but little had happened that night. Now Thena felt a new resolve. Parking her mother's car on the paved road that circled the small Barren cemetery, she turned off the headlights, and the engine. Gathering the items she'd brought with her, she got out, the warm night air soothing her as she entered the graveyard.

Coming here wasn't something she'd been able to contemplate. Once the evening had drawn to a close, it had come to her what she must do. Standing still for just a moment, she stared at the tall and regal yellow poplars that bordered the ground. Well cared-for bluegrass combed the ground, hallowed ground that would aid her in her mission.

She was still full from the supper Priapus had insisted on making for all of them earlier. He'd claimed it was an old tradition, assuring his fair welcome into a household by fixing a meal for everyone. Thena had never heard of such a tradition, even in the ancient societies. Gramma had voiced the same thought, accusing Priapus of making the whole thing up.

He'd grinned roguishly, impressing Gramma so that she almost acted like a schoolgirl around him. Thena rolled her eyes, although couldn't deny the pull he had on her as well. Priapus had the gift to charm, and he'd succeeded wonderfully with her mother and Gramma, having both of them laughing easily at his anecdotes.

Moving among the graves, Thena took a moment to enjoy how the night breeze made the silk fabric of her long black gown brush against her skin. Wearing nothing other than the ceremonial gown, it had been impossible to get out of the house after her mother and grandmother went to sleep without Priapus noticing her.

"You are going out in public dressed like this?" he'd asked when she'd come downstairs after making sure her mother and grandmother slept.

Thena had looked down at her ceremonial gown, the black shiny material swaying enticingly over her body. In the right light it was almost transparent, which was why she liked it. Her magic worked best when she performed it in her natural state, naked, uninhibited by anything of this world. It was the easiest way to become one with the elements around her.

But walking outside without any clothes on wouldn't help her achieve what she needed to do tonight. So she'd donned her ceremonial gown.

"I'm going to the graveyard," she'd told him.

Priapus caressed her breasts, the material torturing her skin as he moved it over her nipples.

"Do you believe this young woman who cursed this town is really buried there?" The way he worded the question let her know he already knew that she wasn't.

And Thena had guessed as much already. Someone dying such a terrible death more than likely would have been buried very privately.

"Come with me if you like. And no, I don't believe that she is. But I do think the guilty parties will come forth if they see me out digging for information."

Priapus had pulled her into his arms, kissing her savagely. "You have a day to figure this out, and then I will step in. This town has suffered enough. Go see what you can learn and know that I'll be watching."

Her lips still tingled from his kiss.

Priapus distracted her thoughts though, and she knew that her magic wouldn't work as well if she couldn't get him off of her mind. Lately though, that had become a terrible chore to master. She was always thinking about him.

Thena sighed, looking around at the quiet, well-kept meadow where their dead had been laid to rest for over a hundred years since the founding of Barren. These were her people, the last names on many of the markers familiar. And she had her mother to thank for that. She'd been given roots, a home to grow up in, people to call her own. Although she'd often felt different from everyone else, those feelings would have intensified if she'd grown up knowing her father was a god.

Her mother had done the right thing. The knowledge burned through her, making her sad, and loving her mother all the more with the acceptance of it.

Knowing what her mother had done brought her to a pivotal point in her life. What was she to do about Priapus? Her mother had chosen a normal life over living with a god. Albeit, witches weren't what many considered normal, but that was their misconception and one she'd learned to live with. Thena had grown up just like everyone else, and had wonderful memories thanks to her mom.

But if she were to settle down with Priapus, have children, how would her family be raised?

Thena shook off the unsettling emotions that sidetracked her from her purpose. She'd come to the cemetery to help her community, not to dwell on her personal feelings and love life.

Night bloomers filled the air with their fresh scent. Potted flowers surrounding well-tended graves added to the aroma. Recently tilled earth added a rich scent that mingled with the other smells. It was a peaceful combination, and she took her time inhaling, focusing on becoming one with her surroundings.

The damp grass soaked through Thena's shoes, and she knew it would make her gown wet as well. Closing her eyes, she allowed herself to float several inches off the ground, working to untie the small pouch she'd brought with her while moving across the sacred ground.

"Wind to the north, spread my charm." She reached into the pouch, filling her hand with the specially mixed faerie dust she needed for her protection spell.

The dust warmed in her hand, its powers seeping through her skin before she cast it to the air around her.

She scattered the powder over the graves as she floated past them. "Moonlight shine the fire from the sun. Warm the hearts of my people. United we are one."

The dust drifted through her fingers, coming to life and shining like hundreds of small streaks of light as it fell over the roots of all of the families in Barren.

"Mother Earth absorb my spell, protect the children of these families and keep them from the evil of hell."

It had occurred to her earlier this evening that this was what she needed to do. After coming to the graveyard the other night with her mother and Gramma, it had occurred to her that almost every family was connected to this sacred ground through their dead loved ones. Her town needed her, and she had the power to save them. By casting her protection spell over the cemetery, focusing on every family who had family here, she would be able to protect anyone else from being possessed by the evil creatures.

She focused on her task, flying from one corner of the graveyard to the next, scattering the powerful faerie dust while whispering words of protection.

"You will be safe, protected from harm." The magical dust scattered over the tombstones.

Slowly the area began glowing from the strength of her magic. Rocks, blades of grass, the graves and their markers, warmed to her power, radiating from her strength.

Her mind was focused, the intensity of her magic rippling through her like waves encouraged by a crisp strong wind. Once done here she would move into the town, making an effort to protect every family, even if they didn't have loved ones in the cemetery.

So intent was she on her spell, on putting an end to the hell that this town had endured, that she didn't sense the man approaching. And when he raised his gun and fired, she was an easy target, struck down in midair.

Priapus could have clobbered Triton for showing up at the most inopportune moment. If he hadn't been distracted into conversation with the god, he would have been able to stop the bullet before it punctured through Thena's flesh.

"No!" he screamed at the same moment that Thena's cries ruptured through the serene setting of the graveyard, scattering her magic across the meadow.

He flew to her faster than any human eye could have followed, grabbing her before she collapsed fully to the ground.

"Hold on, sweetheart." His heart bled at the pained and shocked look in her eyes.

She'd been knocked out of the trance of her spell, which had distracted her too much to prevent her from seeing or stopping her aggressor.

"God. It hurts like hell. Holy shit." She grabbed a hold of Priapus, the sight of him filling her vision, which blurred with the intensity of the pain.

And never had she experienced such intense pain, shooting through her, distracting her too much to figure out where she hurt, or why. All she could see was Priapus, and it didn't make sense to her why he was here, or what he was doing. All she could do was hold on, grab him with all the strength she could muster, while her mind was grossly distracted by stabbing sensations impaling her body.

"It's okay. One second and the pain will be gone." Priapus couldn't stand the confusion that mixed through her.

Thena didn't hate anyone. She would never hurt a soul. And yet she endured the extreme torture of bitter hatred even though she didn't understand it. She had no idea what had just happened to her.

He situated her so that he could get to the bullet hole, a direct hit to her heart. The demon had aimed to kill, and with any other person, his mission would be successful.

But Thena wouldn't die, not tonight, not for a long, long time.

He pressed his fingers against the puncture wound, hating how her brow wrinkled from the pain. Her mouth opened, a scream on her lips, but he moved quickly.

Pushing his fingers into her flesh, reaching into her body, he wrapped his fingers around the bullet and then pulled it out, sealing her wound with a caress of his finger.

"What just happened?" she asked, her face twisting into a sharp grimace as she tried to ease out of the hold he had on her.

"Someone shot you." Priapus pulled her into his arms, silently cursing himself for taking his attention from her for even a moment.

He knew the demons had waited patiently for that small window of opportunity to try and take Thena out.

A scream sounded in the darkness looming beyond the cemetery and Priapus knew that Triton had just destroyed the demon that tried to kill his daughter. In the next moment he returned to join them, floating above the ground next to Priapus who still kept Thena wrapped protectively in his arms.

"You are okay?" Triton looked like he wanted to take her in his own arms, assure himself that his daughter was fine, but he held his ground, making no move to be any closer than he was.

"Yes. I'm fine now." Thena stared into her father's face, seeing his worry and anger crease lines into his forehead and around his eyes. "Someone tried to shoot me."

And it occurred to her that they'd succeeded. Both men nodded silently, giving her the moment she needed to understand what had just happened. She moved just a bit in Priapus' arms, looking down at her bloodstained gown, and knew there was no bullet wound on her body.

"You just saved my life," she said, feeling silly, but immediately having her emotions sated when she looked up into his solemn expression.

Priapus cuddled her into him without answering, and she looked over at her father, hovering very close and looking more than concerned.

He was an attractive man, reminding her of an old sailor. Triton was a sea god so she guessed that made sense. The compassion in his eyes grabbed her though, allowing her to see how terribly much he did care about her. In fact, her father cared enough about her that he'd stayed away so she could grow up normally.

"Thank you," she added, her voice cracking.

She didn't want to be out of Priapus' arms, and now wasn't the time to get chummy with her father. Too much work lay ahead of her, magic best done in the light of the moon.

"The spell is broken though, I'm afraid," she said, looking up at Priapus. "I tried to protect the town, seal it with magic so that no more demons could work their way into the people here."

"Your magic holds fast, my dear," Priapus told her, wiping a bit of faerie dust from her forehead, the strength of the powder making her skin glow. "Your will to protect the families of Barren is all that was needed. I've told you before that your props aren't necessary."

"They are for me." She didn't know if either of them would understand. "No matter what blood courses through my veins, I have to believe to make my magic work. And that belief is stemmed through my rituals. You have to allow me to continue with my work."

"Then allow us to help you," Triton suggested. "Show us how you wish the magic performed and we will honor your ways, assisting in eliminating the demons."

Thena took a moment to understand what her father offered. These two men, these two gods, could wipe out every demon with a mere thought. She was sure of it. Yet Triton offered to do it her way, performing the magic through ritual, through actions.

And the ceremonial actions of eliminating the evil from Barren would help the community too. Thena knew these people. They would see the act, hear about it, talk in hushed whispers with others about what took place on that moonlit night, and it would bond them, adding to the strength of the magic and keep the evil away. Hopefully Priapus and Triton would understand that when dealing with humans, it was best to offer help in a way that they would understand, so they would accept it.

If history was correct at all, Priapus and Triton already knew that this evening would put a barrier between her and her town. Just as it had always done. Something this huge couldn't be ignored. The Barren community would know what she'd done, that her witchcraft, her powers as a goddess, whatever term they wanted to use, had saved their lives. They would be nice to her, and then stay away, until the next time she was needed. And then there would be a silent tap on her back door, as they quietly snuck over to see her, without anyone else knowing they were approaching the village witch.

With a sigh, Thena realized this was how it was meant to be. She was different. And she could live her life fighting it, or she could embrace it, using her gifts to help others when they needed it.

"The three of us could get the task done a lot faster," she admitted, looking up into Priapus' face.

His expression was masked, although the way he held her close, his powerful arms pressing her against his hard body while they hovered over the ground, showed her what he tried to conceal. He had great respect for her father, and wished to gain his approval concerning their bonding as much as he had wanted her mother and Gramma to like him.

"So it shall be." Priapus nodded, consenting that they would work together.

"We fly over the town then," Thena told them, working to straighten herself and hover next to Priapus.

If they were going to work as a team, she would show them how to do things her way. What needed to be done would take a hell of a lot more than simple witchcraft, but they would still do things her way.

"Will your protection on every home, every business, every individual you see on the street," she instructed. "The magic will be its strongest if implemented by moonlight, so there's no time to waste."

Priapus didn't want to let her free. He liked keeping her cuddled next to him, her long black gown fanning around her silky caramel skin. But the intense glow of her brown eyes was enough to see that she was determined to cast out the demons her way.

Reluctantly he allowed her to push herself from his arms, but braced himself to catch her until he was assured she could hover next to him without falling.

Thena couldn't hide the wash of pride that ran through her when she flew alongside Priapus, showing powers that matched his own. The two of them were different, coming from different worlds, but they were soul mates, meant to be. To shatter that would leave them half empty for the rest of their lives. To bond would make them both stronger, more complete than they were on their own.

Her mother had endured loneliness, given up love, and her soul mate, so that Thena would be happy. But her mother's actions didn't have to be Thena's. She would never allow someone to be miserable because of her choices, but letting go of Priapus simply wouldn't be an option.

Taking their time, giving serious attention to their task, she and Priapus moved from home to home, street after street, casting out demons, and protecting those not yet violated. Her powers seemed to boil with a new energy that coursed through her with more strength than her faerie dust ever could offer.

Watching Priapus, feeling his raw untamable power float around him, saturate through her, filled her with an emotion she was sure she'd never experienced before. She had fallen in love with him.

His serious expression when they hovered over a home filled with evil, the determined way he aided in casting out demons, showed her again how much he cared for people.

There were issues. He had a past she wasn't sure about, issues that had hardened his heart. But working together, making eye contact when they knew a house was now rid of the terrible hatred, showed her that that wall around his heart was dissipating.

And by the end of the night, as the moon slowly faded from the sky, and the horizon began to burn with beautiful shades of orange and red, she knew their efforts were a success.

Chapter Seventeen

Priapus stared out the large window, the thick stone walls providing a natural window ledge, and unnecessary protection. Rolling meadows, and snow-capped mountains were part of the beautiful scene that he'd woken up to this morning. The wonderful scent of roses, streaming in through the long sashed curtains, had greeted him when he'd moved to stand and stare at the view outside.

No panes were necessary, the gentle breeze barely moved the thin material that he'd parted in order to see outside. The climate here would always be perfect, as would the walls that he'd designed when he'd built this castle.

Paradise. An absolute utopia. His own sanctuary that had never been complete until he'd brought Thena here.

Turning from the window, his heart swelled at the sight of her buried under blankets on his king-sized bed. One narrow foot stuck out from under the blankets. Her shoulder was exposed, and she'd pulled her hand up to rest next to her cheek.

He knew she would be exhausted. She'd used a level of magic that she'd never touched before. And due to her efforts, with just a little bit of help from him and Triton, she'd successfully cleared Barren of every demon.

That was why he'd brought her here. She needed to rest. Even though his cock throbbed at the sight of her resting in his bed, Priapus knew she would need to sleep in order to build back her strength.

Partially he'd been selfish too. He wanted time alone with her, a lot of time alone with her. And if she'd returned to her mother's home, she'd barely get an hour of sleep before the new day. By now word traveled through the town that everyone had returned to normal. He knew her mother's phone had already rung more than once concerning the matter. Margaret and Gramma would know what happened.

Triton had agreed to tell the older women that Priapus had taken Thena to safe refuge, the location of his castle not something that the women would understand.

"One week," Triton had told him. "I'll give you one week with her and then I want to see her."

Priapus had agreed. He needed more than a week, eternity wouldn't be long enough. But again he knew he was being selfish. Thena had a right to get to know her father, if that was in fact what she wanted to do.

For now she would rest, sleep without interruption until she awoke. Taking one long last look at his sleeping beauty, he walked silently across the large room, disappearing when he reached the doorway.

When Thena awoke, the long shadows filling the room around her didn't look familiar. Wonderfully warm blankets cuddled her in to a perfectly firm mattress. She didn't want to move, or for that matter even wake up. Never had she been so comfortable.

But as she blinked the sleepiness from her eyes, her surroundings grew clearer.

Where in the hell was she?

It took a minute to remember the night before, casting out the demons, flying alongside Priapus while working magic with him.

She sat up in the bed quickly. "Priapus," she called out.

Long, silky transparent fabric draped over a large wooden canopy frame. The four-poster bed was so large someone could have been sleeping with her and she could have stretched without interrupting their slumber. Yet she was alone in the magnificent bed.

Two large windows had long chic drapes that fluttered from a gentle warm breeze. The bed was in the middle of the room, pushed up against the wall opposite the bedroom door, which stood open. She couldn't see past it though, and for the moment was too comfortable to climb out of the bed.

Not to mention the fact that she didn't have any clothing on, and didn't see her clothes anywhere. Hauling any of the thick blankets off of the bed to cover herself so she could explore where she was further sounded like way too much work. Staying put seemed a lot easier at the moment.

"Priapus, where am I?" she whispered this time, seeing no reason to yell for a god who could hear her thoughts.

"In my bed," he whispered back, and then leaned into her.

She jumped in spite of herself, then turned when Priapus wrapped his arms around her, pulling the two of them back on the pile of down pillows. It didn't surprise her to see he wasn't wearing any clothes.

Unable to stop herself, she pulled the covers back, her heart skipping a beat at his enormous cock, bulging and throbbing with promises of lustful satisfaction.

"I'm not sure I'll ever be able to get used to how big you are," she whispered, running her fingers over his thick shaft.

Priapus' head fell back, his hand gripping her shoulder. Just her gentle touch was enough to make him want to throw her down and bury himself deep in her heat. "Take your time and study it all you want," he managed to breathe.

She smiled, nibbling her lower lip while she stroked his cock, testing his size visually by trying to wrap her fingers around it. She wasn't able to. Priapus groaned, and tightened his grip on her.

Feeling a bit of control, although she knew there was no way she could overpower him, physically or magically, Thena moved to her knees, the covers piling around them.

She used both hands, wrapping her fingers around the soft skin that sheathed the iron cock in front of her. His cock head was almost purple, swollen with just a drop of moisture seeping out as she stroked him.

"Come here," he whispered, reaching for her, turning her. "Sit on my face while you play with it."

Now she grinned openly. "You got a deal," she giggled, straddling his head and lowering her cunt to his mouth.

His tongue raked over her eager folds, springing rivers of lust to life as he dipped into her, tasted her. Her sweet scent wrapped around him, hardening him to the point of erotic pain. Never had a woman moved him like this.

Thena's inner thigh muscles stretched as she lowered herself to Priapus' face. His tongue was blissful torture, stroking and teasing her so that she couldn't move, and at the same time wanted to jump up.

With both of her hands she took Priapus' cock, and then leaned forward kissing the moisture from his cock head.

Priapus growled, the vibration trembling through her. She quivered, unable to stop herself, as her first orgasm moved through her. This time he hummed his satisfaction, his tongue lapping at her, drinking the cum he'd induced.

It was all she could do not to clench her legs against the side of his face, smother him with her pussy, and beg him never to stop. She stroked the giant cock throbbing in front of her. There was no way she could take him into her mouth. And at the moment, she wasn't sure she could do anything other than focus on breathing. Even that was a chore.

But she had to offer something in return for the wonderful sensations he was putting her through. Leaning forward, she held on to his cock. She didn't have to move forward very far. His anxious dick bounced up from his chest, greeting her with an eager hello.

Both of her hands wrapped around it, her fingers barely overlapping. The length of him was well over a foot long, swollen and hard as rock. She licked at him as if he were a giant lollipop, running her tongue from one end of his swollen cock head to the other.

Skin so smooth, so soft and so tender, pulsed in her hand. The strength of him, the eager thrust he gave when her tongue touched him, had her aching to give him more.

"Oh baby. Hell yes," Priapus breathed into her pussy, his breath hot and his voice deep and raspy.

She stroked him faster, using her hands and her tongue to soak his shaft. In her wildest dreams she'd never imagined a cock this size. And to think it was hers. More than anything at that moment she knew this to be true. All of him, from giant cock to compassionate god, Priapus was hers.

His tongue impaled her, dipping deep into her folds. Priapus couldn't believe the magic she worked with her tender caresses, her sweet kisses. There was no real magic involved, but her compassion, her concern that he feel the same pleasure that he offered her, made the moment more magical than if they'd combined their powers and altered their bodies.

Her fingers were like soft feathers, moving delicately over his skin, but torturing him as if they were flames burning through his flesh. She stroked and licked his cock until he thought he would explode, emptying himself on her face. And the thought wasn't unappealing. But if he were to come, he wanted to see it happen, watch her expression while he gave her everything he had.

And without a doubt that was what he was doing. Everything he was, everything he had he wanted to give to Thena. The reality of that fact was like a huge burden lifting from his shoulders. No more would he tread through life alone, keep his thoughts to himself, move without the concern of another.

From now on, he was half of a whole. That knowledge felt damned good.

Her fingers moved harder, faster, and she was taking over his ability to think straight.

"Woman," he growled, barely able to contain himself.

He lifted her off of him, catching her satisfied smile, and the glow in her sultry brown eyes when she gazed at him.

"I want to ride you," she whispered, not sure if she could.

She had him so hard. And he was already too large for any woman to be able to handle. But she'd taken him before, and she knew she would enjoy making love to him again and again. One way or another, she would learn how best to fuck this man, this cock that was so unique from any other man's.

"Come here then." He reached for her, seeing the determination on her face. "See how much you can handle."

"I'll always be able to handle all of you," she told him with determination.

"Always?" he asked, needing to hear what he already knew was in her thoughts.

She straddled him, bracing her feet on either side of him and squatting over him. He reached for her hands, holding her, bracing her so that she steadied herself over him, her soaked cunt pressing against the tip of his cock. The heat she soaked him with was too much to bear.

"Always, as in forever," she whispered, and then forced herself down, lowering herself so that his cock stretched her open.

Humidity soared through him as he penetrated her opening, feeling the softness of her folds wrap around him in a loving embrace. So smooth, so hot, so absolutely fucking perfect.

"Forever is a long time," he told her, watching her lashes flutter shut over her eyes, her mouth form a perfect circle as she continued to lower herself over his cock. "But it sounds absolutely wonderful to me."

"Priapus," she began, hardly able to talk.

This position had him impaling her with all that he had, filling her and stretching her unlike she'd ever been filled before.

"Yes?" he asked, aching to hear the words that were on the tip of her tongue.

"I think forever is the perfect amount of time." When she was positive that if she took him another inch he would come up through her mouth, she began rising, feeling the muscles in her legs quiver as he slowly glided out of her. "I have found my soul mate," she added, breathless.

"Yes, you have." And he had found his.

He allowed her a few more times of moving over him, taking all she could and then gliding upwards until he almost left the heat of her insides. Her eyes closed, her mouth barely open, she was the most beautiful sight in the world.

And for the rest of her life, he would enjoy every minute of her. Never had he committed to a woman before. And her being half-goddess made her even more enticing. Together they would explore what life had to offer, grow together and learn from each other. As excited as he was to enjoy that lifetime, he wouldn't rush it, but take it minute by minute. And for now, he would simply relish in her beauty while she showed him how much she loved him.

"I love you, Thena Lotus Cooke," he whispered, and held on to her while she rode him through yet another orgasm.

Epilogue

Thena looked around her empty home, and then turned with a grin when Priapus and Merco entered her front door. Here was where it had all begun, with Priapus walking through her front door in Kansas City. Now he sauntered through, returning her grin, and looking sexy as hell.

"I think we have all of your boxes loaded," Merco said, turning when Naomi entered behind them. He pulled her into his arms. "We both wish you two the best of luck in Kentucky."

"We expect you to visit." Thena held her hand out to Naomi, who took it and offered a friendly squeeze. "I might need your advice from time to time."

Priapus glanced at Merco, and Thena offered them both a knowing smile.

"Well, you have an advantage over me." Naomi let go of Thena's hand and wrapped her arms around Merco's waist. "I don't have any magic at all. It would have taken me days to box up this house."

Thena looked around her. It had been fun using magic to pack everything, watching while her cherished items had floated into boxes. The men had shown off, carrying out boxes with one finger, juggling them once they had them in the large truck parked out front. It was a wonder none of the neighbors had noticed.

That was something she would have to get accustomed to. For years she'd worried about her powers being noticed, about people talking. Yet in just the past few weeks, she'd learned that humans tended to look the other way when they didn't understand something. They would write it off, tell each other it never happened.

Granted, they would always whisper about the time when evil set foot in Barren, and Thena Cooke had come home to set things straight. But they would go on with their lives.

"We'll be down there in a few weeks, after you two are settled," Merco told Priapus.

The four of them exchanged handshakes and hugs, and Naomi and Thena both cried, but Thena knew she would still see her friend a fair bit. Traveling with a god made the distance a lot closer.

Priapus pulled her into his arms, his strength immediately consuming her. His hands brushed over her back, then slid around her, cupping her breasts. She looked up at him, desire rushing through her, as they vanished from her home.

"I think you'll be pleased by this," he whispered in her ear.

Thena would be pleased with both of them out of their clothes, and was about to tell him that, when she realized they had reappeared in the graveyard in Barren. The sensation of having run really fast, and then stopping just as suddenly had her bracing herself. But Priapus was right there, holding on to her.

"What is this?" She looked down at the fresh grave, and the small marker that had recently been placed there.

"Susie Wright was terribly raped and murdered. The horrendous crime allowed the demons to take over this town so easily. They breed on hatred, on fear. Now with the demons gone, those who knew of the crime were able to come forth, have the men arrested, and put Susie to peace in a proper grave."

Thena ran her fingers over the simple stone marker, feeling peace and contentment. She looked up at Priapus. "Why didn't you just wipe out all the evil of Barren when you saw it here?"

Priapus smiled. "If I had, you would never have come to terms with the strength of your powers. And besides, I may be a god, but I'm not God. I don't see everything that is happening everywhere. No god or goddess has that strength."

Thena nodded, knowing there was a lifetime of knowledge before her. "You have enough strength for me."

"I'm glad I'm enough for you," Priapus said, pulling her into his arms, as they faded away once again. "Because you, sweet Thena, are absolutely perfect for me."

About the author:

All my life, I've wondered at how people fall into the routines of life. The paths we travel seemed to be well-trodden by society. We go to school, fall in love, find a line of work (and hope and pray it is one we like), have children and do our best to mold them into good people who will travel the same path. This is the path so commonly referred to as the "real world".

The characters in my books are destined to stray down a different path other than the one society suggests. Each story leads the reader into a world altered slightly from the one they know. For me, this is what good fiction is about, an opportunity to escape from the daily grind and wander down someone else's path.

Lorie O'Clare lives in Kansas with her three sons.

Lorie welcomes mail from readers. You can write to her c/o Ellora's Cave Publishing at 1056 Home Avenue, Akron OH 44310-3502.

Why an electronic book?

We live in the Information Age—an exciting time in the history of human civilization in which technology rules supreme and continues to progress in leaps and bounds every minute of every hour of every day. For a multitude of reasons, more and more avid literary fans are opting to purchase e-books instead of paperbacks. The question to those not yet initiated to the world of electronic reading is simply: *why?*

1. *Price.* An electronic title at Ellora's Cave Publishing and Cerridwen Press runs anywhere from 40-75% less than the cover price of the exact same title in paperback format. Why? Cold mathematics. It is less expensive to publish an e-book than it is to publish a paperback, so the savings are passed along to the consumer.
2. *Space.* Running out of room to house your paperback books? That is one worry you will never have with electronic novels. For a low one-time cost, you can purchase a handheld computer designed specifically for e-reading purposes. Many e-readers are larger than the average handheld, giving you plenty of screen room. Better yet, hundreds of titles can be stored within your new library—a single microchip. (Please note that Ellora's Cave and Cerridwen Press does not endorse any specific brands. You can check our website at www.ellorascave.com or

www.cerridwenpress.com for customer recommendations we make available to new consumers.)

3. *Mobility.* Because your new library now consists of only a microchip, your entire cache of books can be taken with you wherever you go.
4. *Personal preferences are accounted for.* Are the words you are currently reading too small? Too large? Too...**ANNOYING**? Paperback books cannot be modified according to personal preferences, but e-books can.
5. *Instant gratification.* Is it the middle of the night and all the bookstores are closed? Are you tired of waiting days—sometimes weeks—for online and offline bookstores to ship the novels you bought? Ellora's Cave Publishing sells instantaneous downloads 24 hours a day, 7 days a week, 365 days a year. Our e-book delivery system is 100% automated, meaning your order is filled as soon as you pay for it.

Those are a few of the top reasons why electronic novels are displacing paperbacks for many an avid reader. As always, Ellora's Cave and Cerridwen Press welcomes your questions and comments. We invite you to email us at service@ellorascave.com, service@cerridwenpress.com or write to us directly at: 1056 Home Ave. Akron OH 44310-3502.

ELLORA'S CAVE
ROMANTICA PUBLISHING